# PAGES AND CO.

# THE

# LAST BOOKWANDERER

*The Pages & Co. series*

# Pages and Co.
## THE
# LAST BOOKWANDERER

# ANNA JAMES

### ILLUSTRATED BY
## MARCO GUADALUPI

PHILOMEL

PHILOMEL
An imprint of Penguin Random House LLC, New York

First published in Great Britain by HarperCollins Children's Books, 2023
First published in the United States of America by Philomel,
an imprint of Penguin Random House LLC, 2024

Visit us online at PenguinRandomHouse.com.

Library of Congress Cataloging-in-Publication Data is available.

ISBN 9780593327265

1st Printing

Printed in the USA

LSCH

US edition edited by Cheryl Eissing. • US edition designed by Ellice M. Lee.
Text set in Adobe Caslon Pro.

*For my grandad, who is part of all my stories,*

*even these that he is not here to read*

# 1

## A Tangle of History and Myth

W hen traveling through a magical portal, you don't usually expect to end up at a tourist attraction. And yet, for five bookwanderers, that was exactly what seemed to have happened. They stood beneath a slate archway and behind them stretched the wilds of the Northumbrian countryside. In front of them was somewhere entirely different—instead of fields, there was the sea, but there was also a queue of slightly sunburned people staring at them in annoyance. Thankfully, these people didn't seem to be able to see Northumberland through the portal, or the magical book-smuggling train waiting there. The dirty looks were all due to Tilly, Milo, Oskar, Alessia, and Rosa jumping the queue for the archway photo opportunity.

"The portal is broken," Alessia said bluntly.

"It's not exactly broken," Oskar pointed out. "It did bring us . . . somewhere. Something magical happened."

"It took us to the right place," Rosa said slowly, looking around. "This is Tintagel Castle in Cornwall all right. But I'm worried that it's the wrong time—or the wrong . . . layer?"

"It's me," said Milo, resigned. "I did something wrong. I'm not the Anonymous Reader after all. I've created some sort of sightseeing portal instead of the one we need to find *The Book of Books*. The Alchemist is going to track it down first, steal everyone's imagination, and it's all my fault."

"Well, can we go back and try again?" Tilly asked, just as the hazy gateway shimmered out of existence.

"You ruined it," Alessia said accusingly to Tilly.

"I hardly think a stone archway is listening to me," Tilly retorted. "Is it?" She turned to Rosa, who looked troubled.

Considering Rosa was the person who was closest to being in charge, this wasn't the most reassuring thing for the others to see.

"Hang on, though," said Oskar. "What did you say about layers? You said we might be in the wrong time or the wrong layer?"

"I'm not sure how the magic is supposed to work," admitted Rosa. "There's never been any serious threat to the Book before the Alchemist learned of its existence, and I can't use the gateway by myself, so I haven't been here before. I was taught how to get here, but not what to do next. I must say I thought it would be more obvious. We seem to have come to actual Tintagel Castle in the regular world—the portal has simply teleported us. I was expecting it to take us inside Story, or even back in time. Merlin isn't exactly going to be wandering around in jeans, taking selfies and queuing for ice cream, is he?"

"Is he not?" Oskar asked entirely sincerely. "Fictional people are rarely what you're expecting."

"Well, I suppose I don't know," Rosa said, sounding flustered. "I've never met him before! Maybe he's immortal, and has hung out here for centuries and just carries the Book around in a backpack!"

The four younger bookwanderers looked at Rosa, worried. Before the Alchemist had taken Pages & Co. hostage, Rosa had rarely become visibly frazzled and always seemed confident as to the best thing to do. The news that the Alchemist had discovered a secret route to *The Book of Books*—via a book hidden in Pages & Co.—had turned her focused determination into scattered fear.

"It's not your fault, you know," Milo said gently. "None of it."

"Is it not, sweet Milo?" she replied with a sad smile.

"It's not," Tilly said firmly.

When she had first learned that Rosa had known all along that the Book was at Pages & Co. and hadn't warned her family, she'd felt quite differently. But despite her fear for her family, she knew there was only one place to lay the blame.

"My grandad would say that even if we make mistakes in how we react, bad things are always the fault of the person acting badly in the first place."

"That sounds very wise," Rosa said. "But I'm not sure it's so clear-cut in this case. The whole purpose of my life and work is to protect *The Book of Books*, and now not only is it in danger, but your family are being used as collateral because of my decisions."

"The only reason any of that's happening is because my father is evil," Alessia said with a resigned sigh. "Which sounds very dramatic, but it's true, and if I can make peace with that, then so can all of you. He's holding Tilly's family and Milo's uncle prisoner because he wants the secrets of the Book and because he wants to enslave the whole world's imagination. Now, I suggest that we stop debating all of this and get on with finding Merlin, or finding our way to the same layer of Story that he's in."

"You're right," said Rosa with a sharp nod. "Thank you, Alessia. We have a mission, and the only way to rescue your families is to complete it."

She took another step away from the queue of photo-takers and frowned in concentration, but Milo could see that the worry and responsibility she felt were simply tucked away temporarily, not gone.

The group took in their surroundings more thoroughly. They were standing in the ruins of a very old castle on an almost-island, only connected to the mainland by a huge tumble of rocks and a shiny, modern bridge. A meter or so away from where they stood was a sharp drop down to a small sandy cove. The salty air and sunshine were a small balm to their worries, and the sight of the sea meeting the sky will always bolster an adventurous heart. A friendly-looking woman in an English Heritage gilet came over to them and smiled encouragingly at Rosa.

"School group?" she asked.

"Huh?" replied Rosa in confusion.

"You seem a little lost," the woman said, "so I was just wondering if I could maybe point you to what you're after. Are you looking for the rest of your group? I didn't realize we had a school trip in today—or are you home educators? All welcome! Anyway, school groups are often looking for the Dark Ages ruins up on the headland. Or the Tristan and Isolde myth garden." She said all this very quickly and left Rosa looking a little stunned.

"Thank you!" Tilly said, jumping in. Only she and Oskar actually had any experience of regular school; the other three were entirely unfamiliar with the rhythms of a school trip. "We're actually researching Merlin for a class project, so if you could point us to the stuff about him, that would be amazing."

"Of course!" the woman said kindly, looking delighted to be able to help. "Well, Merlin's Cave, down below in the cove, is the part of the site named after him, but he was integral to King Arthur's birth, which took place right here in the castle. Well, sort of. There wasn't technically a castle here back when that was supposed to have happened, more a settlement. This place is a bit of a tangle of history and myth, but I think that's what makes it so special. Merlin was Arthur's guide, as I'm sure you know if you're doing a project on him. Have you been up to take a look at the sculpture at the top? Definitely worth seeing that if it's Arthurian myths you're learning about! Just follow the signs! And it's down the steps to the cave. We're closing in an hour, though, so do make sure you leave enough time to see everything you want!"

"Thanks so much," Oskar said, and he and Tilly encouraged the other three along the path that led away from the bridge, farther out onto the headland.

Despite the sunshine, the wind was bracing on the exposed coast, and the farther they got from the bridge, the wilder the land became. They passed more remnants of civilizations past that reminded Milo of the remains of Hadrian's Wall. As the path led them upward, a grid of mossy stones came into view, and a sign told them that they had been built back in the Dark Ages, the period after the Romans left Britain. There was even a kiln made of slate in one corner where medieval people would have dried out their corn.

"It's wild thinking of all the different sorts of people who've lived here, isn't it?" Oskar said, staring at the kiln as though he could see back into the past.

"Yeah, it feels like we're moving through layers of history just by walking here, never mind layers of Story," agreed Tilly.

"They're not so dissimilar in the end," said Rosa. "History is a story in many ways—the archeologists and historians who dug these buildings up had to create narratives to connect the evidence they found and make sense of it. We rarely, if ever, know exactly what happened in the past, especially when we're looking this far back. And that's not even taking into consideration the fact that most of the stuff we do find belonged to the richest or most important people. Lots of ordinary people couldn't write for great swaths of history, so we don't have any of their letters or diaries, and no one was paying much attention to what normal people were doing anyway. And Tintagel is a place where stories and history get even more muddled than usual because it's a place of myths and legends, as well as real people. For a long time, many believed that the stories about King Arthur and Merlin were actual history."

"Hang on, King Arthur isn't real?" Tilly asked, feeling as though she should have known that.

"I would have thought you of all people knew that the boundary between real and imaginary is more than a bit squishy, Tilly," said Rosa gently, "given your half-fictional nature."

Tilly smiled ruefully. "Sure, but I'm hardly King Arthur. People won't be writing books about me."

"Who's to say they won't?" said Rosa, smiling. "But, taking your question at face value, truly we don't really know and probably never will. Certainly, the stories that people like Geoffrey of Monmouth and Tennyson—"

"And Thomas Malory," Oskar interrupted.

"Yes, exactly," Rosa said.

"How do you know that?" Alessia asked, impressed.

"I'm pretty into King Arthur stuff," Oskar said with a shrug. "I loved the TV show *Merlin*, and then I read a graphic-novel version of the myths, which was adapted from the Malory book."

"How come you didn't mention that before?" Tilly asked. "Like on the train when we found out we were coming to find Merlin?"

"Well, because there was a lot going on!" Oskar said. "It was more important to look after you because of the whole just-found-out-my-family-is-being-held-prisoner thing, and we needed to get back to the treehouse, and then it was much more important to look after Milo after the Alchemist poisoned his grandmother. My pop-culture habits didn't seem relevant—and I figured I could chime in as necessary."

"I'm certainly very glad to have another Arthurian enthusiast on the team," Rosa said. "As you must know then, all the stories those people wrote are understood to be essentially fiction these days—not that it makes them any less important. And I think we might learn much more from them in our fight against the Alchemist than in regular, straightforward history."

"How do you know all this if you've never been here before?" Alessia asked.

"Because I read," Rosa replied with a smile. "Just like Oskar does. The whole world, and beyond, is open to you if you read. I've been to many, many places I've never set foot in before, as I'm sure you have too. And, when it comes to this sort of thing specifically, I'm sure you can imagine I'm particularly well versed on anything to do with Merlin, given his role as the keeper of *The Book of Books*. But, regardless, I'm fairly certain the official line these days is that there's not much history to back it all up besides an obscure mention of an ancient king in an old manuscript—I'm sure that friendly lady by the arch could tell us the up-to-date academic thinking on it all, but some people, myself included, would posit that all myths are rooted in something real. And who am I to say where the line lies between the real and the imaginary—or who can bend it?"

# 2

## Gallos

Right then, shall we have a look at this sculpture while we're up here and then head down to the cave?" Rosa suggested as they approached a jut of rock. Another shorter queue of people waiting to take photos made the sculpture easy to find.

Standing on a flat rocky outcrop that gave Milo the heebie-jeebies, the sculpture was a towering, ghostly-looking thing that made Milo feel strange in an entirely different kind of way. It wasn't clear what it was made of—some kind of metal with a greenish, weather-beaten tinge. It took the shape of a man in a cape wearing a crown and holding a sword, but it had gaps in it so you could see the sky and the sea and the rocks through it. Tilly was the shortest of their group, and it looked nearly double the height of her.

"Is it supposed to be like that?" asked Oskar, pointing at the gaps.

"Oh yes," Rosa said. "It was designed like that. I've only seen photos of it before, but it's quite something when you're in front of it, isn't it?"

She was right—there was a sense of majesty and danger that emanated from the sculpture, and Milo felt half drawn to it and half intimidated by it.

"So, who is it?" Alessia asked. "King Arthur?"

"It's called *Gallos*," Rosa answered. "It comes from the Cornish word for 'power.' It's not supposed to be one person in particular, but I think it's fair to say it certainly represents elements of King Arthur. But also all the ancient kings of this place, and the people of power who have passed through."

"So Merlin too?" Milo asked.

"Do you see Merlin in him?" said Rosa.

"I don't know what Merlin looks like," pointed out Milo.

"Does anyone?" Rosa replied. "But I think if it makes you think of Merlin, then that's what matters. Art doesn't have a set meaning."

"Well, obviously we think it looks like Merlin," Alessia said matter-of-factly. "Because that's who we're looking for, so we're going to see clues in everything."

Milo took a step closer, feeling hypnotized by the sculpture.

"Do you see something, Milo?" Rosa asked him, paying close attention.

"Ohhhh, is an Anonymous Reader thing happening?" Alessia said excitedly.

"Oh no, no," he said, embarrassed. "Please don't think that every time I look at something there's anything special and magical going on. You'll just be disappointed."

But it was too late, and the others had already clustered around the sculpture, on the hunt for any clue as to where they might find Merlin.

"Merlin?" Alessia whispered, which gave Oskar the giggles.

It was Tilly who noticed just how uncomfortable Milo looked, and she stepped backward, pulling him gently to one side.

"I know how it feels," she said, "everyone thinking everything you do means something. Or expecting you to be able to figure things out just because you have something unusual about you."

"I went from being a normal . . . Well, not quite normal, I suppose," Milo admitted. "Arguably, nowhere even close, given I grew up on a magical train with only my uncle and fictional characters for company. But I went from being nothing special to Someone with a capital 'S.' And I feel responsible for us being able to find Merlin and rescuing Horatio and your family—and we've not even finished the cure yet, and I haven't really stopped to think about . . ." He tailed off.

"About your grandmother?" said Tilly gently.

"Yes," said Milo. It was only about an hour ago that they'd gotten back to Rosa's treehouse to discover that Lina, the grandmother Milo had only just found, had been poisoned by the Alchemist. "I know she wasn't a good person, that she betrayed us all, but she was still family, and I'd barely had the chance to speak to her about anything. I wanted to ask her about my parents and her memories, but now she's gone."

"I know that lots of things about our families are different," Tilly said, "so I'm not saying that we feel the same, or that I know exactly what you're going through. But I do know what it's like not to know your parents. I never met my father, and my mother was missing for the first eleven years of my life."

"At least you got her back," Milo said, and then felt bad. "I'm sorry. It's not about who's had it worst."

"You don't need to apologize," Tilly said kindly. "I still can't believe that I got her back, and it meant I had a happy ending, but I just wanted to say that I know a little bit of what it's like, and I'm here anytime you want to talk about your grandmother. We're going to work out a way to save both our families, I promise."

Milo tried to quash the feeling of uncertainty that came over him when he thought about Horatio and his future. But that was a problem for a later time. Right now, there was only one thing to do and that was to find Merlin and make sure *The Book of Books* was safe.

Tilly looked back at the group, who were still studying the sculpture as a group of tourists behind them tutted and conspicuously checked their watches.

"Thank you," Milo said. "I'm glad you're here."

Tilly smiled. "You too. I'm glad we're all here. Between us, we'll work it out, I'm sure of it."

Milo and Tilly convinced the others that there was nothing magical going on with the sculpture, and they started following the path back round the cliffside to get down to the cove. As they rounded the bend, Milo glanced behind him, and for a fraction of a second, he thought he saw a shimmer of iridescence pass over the sculpture. He rubbed his eyes and it was gone, and he put it down to the wind and the sand and the sky playing tricks on him.

The trail led them back to the archway and the old castle, but instead of directing them over the bridge, the signs pointed them to a gnarled wooden door set into the slate wall. Steep and uneven stone steps curved down from it, clinging to the cliffside and then crossing under the bridge and leading down to the beach. The thin strip of land that kept the outcrop from becoming a proper island had clearly been worn down over the centuries, but now it was just tumbled rocks and weatherworn cliff.

"It looks like a giant has taken his foot to it," Oskar said, peering over the handrail to look at the huge boulders that lay on both sides.

"Maybe one did," Alessia said—and, not for the first time, Tilly wasn't sure if she was being sincere or sarcastic.

Tilly had almost immediately liked and trusted Milo a great deal, but she was still a little more cautious around Alessia. Not because Tilly was worried that she was working for her father in any capacity, but because her sense of humor and view on the world were so different from anyone she had ever encountered before. Then again, Alessia had saved her and Oskar's lives at least once before, and that counted for a lot from any perspective.

Where the steps met the opposite cliff, there was a tiny gift shop tucked into a corner.

"Oh, a gift shop! Can we go in?" asked Oskar in delight, his eyes lighting up.

"Right now?" Tilly replied in surprise. "When the whole world's imagination and several family members are at risk?"

"Oh yes, sorry," Oskar said sheepishly. "I just love a gift shop—I got caught up in the moment. I love all this mythology stuff. Or rather I would love it if we were here on holiday," he corrected.

"I mean, the person working there might have some useful Merlin information?" Milo said, feeling bad for Oskar. "Five minutes won't make a difference in the grand scheme of things."

"Fine!" Tilly said, sounding exasperated. "But if it turns out that—Oh, look, fridge magnets!"

They spent a very happy five minutes in the gift shop,

knighting each other with the wooden swords, and trying on the plastic crowns. Tilly bought a little metal fridge magnet of the castle.

"For our kitchen when all this is over," she said firmly. "When Pages & Co. is free, I'm going to go and put this on our fridge and eat dinner with my family."

"An excellent idea," Alessia said. "It would be naive of me to buy a fridge magnet, given I have no home to return to, but I shall get this wooden sword. If someone could lend me the money?" She looked optimistically at Rosa, who laughed and bought them all one.

"We're not too old for these?" Tilly asked, checking how the others were treating theirs. "They are toys after all."

"Firstly, no one is too old for play," Rosa replied. "And secondly, given who we're looking for, I don't think having a weapon of some sort is the worst thing in the world. Even a wooden one."

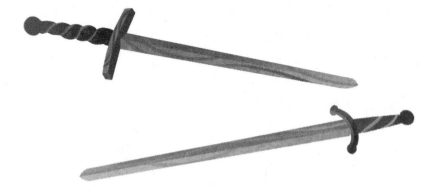

"Sorry, miss, is everything okay?" the gift shop assistant asked at that. "Are you lot in trouble? Those swords can't do any damage, but that's how it should be. You can't go around giving children weapons."

"Ah, sorry, sir," Rosa said, flushing. "Just messing about. I meant . . ."

"She meant that we're going to meet my uncle on the beach," said Milo quickly, "and he's promised us a battle."

"Ahhh," the man said, clearly relieved. "Of course! Do remember to watch out for the tides, though—they come in quicker than you'd think in the cave, and the sea's on its way back up. Don't go too far in if you don't want to get caught out. It's very embarrassing to have to be rescued. But off you go, and I wish you well with your battle! May your swords be worthy!"

# 3

# I Wish We'd Worn Wellies

The beat of normality and the concern of the gift shop assistant provided a brief but welcome respite from the intensity of the situation, and though the wooden swords swinging at their waists felt a little silly, they also gave them all a touch more courage, even if they wouldn't admit it to each other. Milo reminded himself that he'd managed to wield the vorpal sword and defeat the Jabberwock when they were hunting for the ingredients for the cure to wake Horatio up. At the very least, a well-placed wooden sword could be used to trip some-body up, he thought.

At the end of the steps, there was a bit of a clamber down some rocks, and then they were on the beach. Children were splashing and screaming in the chilly water, while parents watched with coffees, towels at the ready, trying to lure them out. It was late afternoon, and although the sun was far from setting, families were starting to pack their things up, ready to head back to holiday cottages and camper vans, to wash the sand off and get the barbecue going.

"Does the beach close?" Milo asked, worried.

"I don't think you can close a beach," Alessia answered, as practical as ever. "You could close access to it, I suppose. But I'm pretty sure we're up to climbing over a gate if we need to. Given what we've already dealt with, a little light trespassing is no big deal. Hey, Oskar, did I tell you about when me and Tilly and Milo jumped out of a window into a canal to escape my father? It was amazing! I felt like an action star."

"It was actually terrifying," Tilly chimed in.

"In the moment, sure," Alessia said. "But, you know, I'd always wanted to say that I'd jumped out of a window."

"Really?" Oskar laughed.

"Doesn't everyone?"

"Can't say I ever gave it any thought," said Oskar. "But I would be telling as many people as possible that story if I'd been there."

"There's a fairly limited number of people you could tell it to," Tilly pointed out.

"I'll just have to write my memoirs one day," Oskar said with a grin, and Milo was struck by how much more manageable everything seemed when you were with friends.

While not visible from the castle up above, the yawning entrance of Merlin's Cave was impossible to ignore from sea level. An eerie dark chasm altered the mood of the pretty beach, and that same mood settled over the bookwanderers as they picked their way across the sand to its entrance.

"It goes all the way through!" Oskar exclaimed, and he was right: the cave was more of a tunnel, eating its way right through the cliff underneath the castle. There was a crescent of light that shone through from the other side, lighting the spray rising from the water into a glowing mist.

The group approached the entrance, which was empty except for a couple taking photographs. Although the tide was about level with the entrance, with the occasional wave making its way in, there was still a wide expanse of stones and sand clear of the water.

"Careful," one of the couple said, "the tide's coming in, and it comes in faster than you'd think."

"Thank you," Rosa said politely, but kept walking forward.

The cave started to narrow in width as they went deeper, and it was harder to find a route through the damp sand and uneven rocks. They could hear water splashing farther down, the sea coming into sight as they followed the curve of the cave.

"Are you sure there wasn't anything in the guardian of *The Book of Books* manual about what to do next?" Oskar asked.

"There really should be a manual, shouldn't there?" Rosa said. "I'm hoping something will become obvious. I tell you what: if we get out of this alive, then I'm going to have you all help me write one to pass on to my successor."

"Uh, there's a chance we won't get out alive?" Oskar repeated in horror.

"Did you not realize?" Alessia said, giving Oskar a pat on the arm. "Peril levels are extremely high. But let's remain optimistic for now. We got here before my father, and I imagine the level will rise once he works out how to get here from Pages & Co."

Rosa was climbing tentatively up some large and slippery rocks on one side of the cave. The couple taking photos were watching in concern.

"The tide really is coming in fast!" one of them shouted.

"Don't worry, we're keeping an eye out!" Oskar called back. "I'm going to go and stand by the entrance to actually keep watch on the sea," he added more quietly. "We really don't want to get trapped in here."

"Good idea," said Alessia. "I'll come with you and look for clues."

"You really don't have to," Oskar said.

"I think it's for the best," Alessia insisted. "I'm more attuned to looking for clues and suchlike than any of you, apart from Rosa." The other three children started to protest before accepting that she was right.

Oskar and Alessia picked their way back to the entrance to reassure the couple they were paying attention to the tide, and to look for clues. Rosa was high up on the rocks, feeling around in dark, damp corners that neither Tilly nor Milo much relished the thought of exploring.

"I don't know what we're looking for," Tilly whispered

to Milo. "Did you get much of a look at that symbol we both touched? The one by the portal?"

"I didn't think to look closely," Milo admitted. "I was a bit overwhelmed. But it was sort of . . . swirly, right? A bit like a labyrinth?"

"Yeah, that's about all I've got. Three swirls, I think, but there might have been four? I guess that's the only thing I can think to look for—or feel for," Tilly said with a shudder. "I really hope there's nothing with too many legs hiding in any of these pools." She started tentatively running her fingers along the rock face and into its crevices. "I've never been one for caves." She looked nervously at her feet, where there was a distinct layer of water now. "I wish we'd worn wellies."

"It's just like being in *The Railway Children*," Milo said, trying to convince himself as much as Tilly.

"What do you mean?"

"You know that the Railway Children are my comfort-blanket characters," Milo said, smiling at the memory of the conversation he and Tilly had had on the top of the Quip about that very subject. "Well, there's a scene in the book where they see some boys racing through a tunnel, but one doesn't come out the other end, and they know there's a train coming, so they have to go in and rescue him. I don't go to that bit much because it's pretty scary, but I've visited a few times. Anyway, that tunnel is much longer and darker, and not much less damp, and it also has a train coming through at top speed. So I much prefer this one."

"I like that," Tilly said. "Did you . . . did you say that your grandmother had told you *The Railway Children* was Horatio's comfort-blanket book too just before—"

"Yes," Milo said, interrupting her before she finished the sentence. "She did. I guess me and Horatio have more in common than I realized. So that's where I need to go to get the last ingredient for the cure—what we can use instead of the Records that were destroyed."

"Do you know what you need from the story?" Tilly asked.

"I'm hoping it will become obvious, but that approach isn't getting us very far currently!" He gave a brief mirthless laugh. "But I can worry about that once we know the Book is safe."

"We'll work it out," Tilly said. "I'm sure."

"I hope so," Milo said. "Because it—"

"Oh!" Tilly shouted, interrupting him. She held up a bleeding finger.

"Are you okay?" called Rosa, slipping down the rocks as fast as she could.

"Yes, fine," Tilly said, sucking her finger to stop the blood and kneeling down on the damp sand, not worrying about her hair trailing in the seawater, which was definitely slightly deeper than it had been a few minutes ago. Tilly had her head nearly on the sand, so she could look underneath a shelf of rock that was jutting out at about waist height. She unfolded herself and grinned up at Rosa and Milo.

"Swirls!" she announced triumphantly.

# 4

## Let Me Tell You a Story

As Tilly stood up, knees damp, Oskar and Alessia rejoined them.

"The sea really is coming in quite quickly," Oskar said anxiously, and the group looked down at their feet, where the seawater was pooling. "My socks are wet."

"We'll be quick," Rosa promised. "But Tilly's found something."

"Under that rock," Tilly added, pointing.

"I'll take your word for it," said Oskar.

"So, what do we do now?" asked Alessia, who had immediately launched herself onto her knees so she could see underneath properly. "There's something else in here too, I think?" She reached an arm under the rock and felt around. "There's like a . . . button maybe? Or a very small handle? I can feel a ring of something that I can't move."

"Can I have a look?" Rosa asked, kneeling down and

immediately soaking the bottom half of her dungarees. "Do any of you have your phone on you, and could you shine a light down here?"

"I'm saving my battery," Tilly said. "In case I hear from anyone at Pages & Co."

"Of course," Rosa said immediately.

"Here," Oskar volunteered, pulling his phone out of his pocket and turning the flashlight on. He crouched down and shone it under the ledge.

"There is something glinting in there," Rosa said. "At the back."

"Is it just a worn bit of rock or something?" Oskar suggested.

"No, it's too regular in shape," Alessia said, crawling farther in, seemingly unbothered by the rising water that was swirling around her. "It's a perfect circle—and it looks like gold to me. I can't . . . get it . . . out . . . though," she grunted as she yanked at the ring.

"Me neither," Rosa said, squeezing in next to Alessia under the ledge. "I can just about get a grip on it, but it's wedged right into the stone—I think we'd need tools to get it out. But could it be a button or trigger? Does it activate something?"

"And this is definitely right?" Oskar said a little skeptically, glancing back at the cave entrance. "I really think we need to get going. Maybe we could find somewhere to stay around here, or try and get back to the treehouse and come back tomorrow?"

"I just think it's too much of a coincidence that the portal brought us to Tintagel, this cave is named after Merlin, and now we've found his symbol in here," Rosa said, an edge of desperation entering her voice. "It's the same symbol as on the archway—a triskele. An ancient druidic symbol—it stands for movement, cycles, revolution, that sort of thing. We just need to work it out quickly. Or else we'll go. I promise. Now, Milo, do you want to try touching the circle?" Rosa edged back out, a little breathless. "Or the triskele, or maybe both at the same time?"

"I will, of course," he said. "But be ready for absolutely nothing to happen."

He felt self-conscious as he crouched down in the water, immediately getting his trousers soaked. The water was past their ankles now, and it was cold. He scooted under the ledge a little, trying to think of the Railway Children in the tunnel as he moved into the dark, struggling to put tentacles and poisonous spines out of his mind.

Feeling for the triskele, he pushed his hand firmly on it, just as he had when he opened the portal in Hadrian's Wall. Nothing happened, just as he was expecting. Feeling with his other hand on the slimy wall, he found the ridge of the golden ring. He could just about put his hands on both at the same time with his arms outstretched and, feeling ridiculous, he touched a finger to each simultaneously. Still nothing. But then . . . he felt the golden ring move a little. Just a tiny shift—but definitely something.

"Did you say the ring was stuck fast?" he asked as a wave lapped uncomfortably high around his waist, his jumper getting heavy and cold.

"Yes," Alessia said. "Maybe try rubbing it or something? Aladdin's-lamp-style."

"It's not . . . Is it a problem if . . ." The ring was definitely not wedged into the wall. In fact, it was so loose that it was about to . . .

*Oh no*, Milo thought to himself as the ring slipped cleanly out of the rock, straight into the roiling waves.

As he desperately fumbled in the churned-up sand and water for it, there was a pulse of something that shook the whole cave. The sound of rocks tumbling and *splashing into the water* was unmistakable, and suddenly four pairs of hands grabbed him and pulled him out from under the ledge, so quickly that he scratched his cheek on the rock. The five of them huddled together, up to their knees in salty water, and looked around as another pulse of energy shuddered through the cave, *sending jets of misty spray up into the air*, illuminated by the late-afternoon sun.

"Did I break something?" Milo fretted, holding out the ring on his palm to show the others. It was a thick gold band, with a very dark red stone set into it.

"No," said a deep voice from behind them. "It was simply waiting for the right person to remove it. It's a favorite trick of mine, actually."

The five very damp bookwanderers turned to see a tall, elderly man standing on a rock that was encircled by seawater. He had a long white beard that was plaited and tied with a leather cord strung with a triskele symbol. Heavy gray robes billowed out around him as the wind whipped through the cave, and a thick hood nearly covered his eyes. He clasped a carved wooden staff in one hand, and a long sword hung in a scabbard from his waist.

"Merlin?" Rosa breathed as they all stared up at him, the swirling seawater temporarily forgotten.

He nodded, lifted his staff, and slammed it into the rock he was standing on.

"Let me tell you a story," he said.

# 5

## Begin at the End

Another pulse of energy rippled through the cave, even more powerful than the last. It sent beams of iridescent light shooting out from Merlin's staff, lighting the crevices of the tunnel and reflecting off the eddying water. It reached the edges of the tunnel before Merlin struck the rock again, then was sucked back into the gnarled carving at the end of his staff.

For a brief moment, everything was utter darkness.

When light returned, it wasn't the same rich late-afternoon sun that had been there before, but a hazy early-morning light, cold with salt and frost. As this new light stretched its fingers through the tunnel, the seawater started rushing backward, as though a plug had been pulled in a bath. Rocks that were on the ground tumbled back upward into the rock face, and the sand become powdery under their feet. The bookwanderers breathed a sigh of relief as the water receded, but that relief was quickly replaced by a distinctly unpleasant feeling as their damp clothes flapped against their cold skin. They were shivering within seconds as the sharp wind whirled through the tunnel.

Merlin simply gestured with his staff at the wall to his right, and towering shadows started to flicker across the rocks, like intricate paper puppets lit from behind.

"Let us begin at the end," Merlin said, and the silhouette of a man and a woman standing by a tree flared into existence. "At the close of my story, at least the one that people tell, I had my magic taken from me by the beautiful Lady Nimue, the enchantress to whom I had taught all that I knew, and the woman that I loved."

The shadow moved as he spoke, a great circle opening at the base of the tree and swallowing up the man before closing again—the woman evaporating into a curl of smoke.

"I knew that this was my fate, but I was powerless to stop it, even as she led me to this tree and opened its roots to seal me under it forever. Now let us go further back in time, and we will see where we end up."

From there, the shadows on the wall told tales of quests and battles and great courtly romances, as beautiful ladies and gallant knights flitted in the light, and Merlin told stories of daring, betrayal, love, and magic. The bookwanderers stood, their shivers forgotten, as Merlin wove his history for them, the shadows seeming more real than the cold and the wind in the cave.

Milo had never read any Arthurian myths, so these great heroes were being introduced to him for the first time, but the others felt their pulses rise as they saw familiar stories come to life on the wall in front of them. The Green Knight, Lancelot, Guinevere . . . all of them featured in Merlin's tapestry. Whole histories were told, but the sharp light of sunrise never wavered, and the tide never washed in or out.

An image of a great rock and an anvil with the handle of a sword appeared, but Merlin waved his hand, and it dissipated into smoke.

"We'll come to that," he said, and glanced at Tilly. "For we have come back to where it all began—above us in the castle at Tintagel."

On the wall, a headland easily identifiable as Tintagel shimmered into life, and a grand castle with turrets and flags overlooking the sea appeared. On the battlements a finely dressed woman stood, staring out to sea, hair blowing in the wind. A second castle appeared, one with a battle raging beneath it. The bookwanderers watched as a man wearing a crown left the battle and galloped on his horse toward Tintagel.

"That is King Uther Pendragon," Merlin said. "One of the legendary kings of the Britons. He was in love with Lady Igraine, but she was already wed. And so he came to me for aid, and I disguised him as the lady's husband, Gorlois."

At this, the crown on the head of the shadow melted away, his hair grew, and he shifted into the shape of a different man, who was let into the castle of Tintagel without challenge. They watched as Igraine ran to meet him and kissed him.

"Unbeknownst to either of them, the true Gorlois was by this point already dead," Merlin went on. "He had seen Uther leave the battle and tried to chase him, but was caught up in the fighting and perished. But Uther and Igraine were enchanted by my magic, and Igraine became pregnant. When the news of Gorlois's death reached them, Uther married Igraine."

"I'm sorry to interrupt," Tilly said nervously. The shadows stopped their dance, as if someone had pressed pause.

"What, child?" Merlin said, sounding more than a little annoyed.

"I just . . . Did you just say that you tricked Igraine into thinking she was with her husband, but it was actually somebody else?"

"Aye?" Merlin said, confused. "Were the shadows not clear enough?"

"But . . ." Tilly tapered off, looking at the others in confusion. "Isn't this guy the hero?" she whispered, looking warily up at Merlin.

"I'll admit that the Arthurian myths aren't very good on feminism," Oskar said. "My graphic-novel version kind of skimmed over this bit."

"Uther was weak for love with Igraine," Merlin said.

"But how did Igraine feel about Uther?" Alessia asked.

"I do not know," Merlin said, perplexed. "They seemed

perfectly content together afterward to me. Why do you hinder me with these questions? Igraine's feelings are not part of this story."

The four children looked at Rosa for guidance. She seemed perturbed.

"May I continue?" Merlin asked, but it was clear he wasn't interested in their permission.

"Of course," Rosa said loudly to Merlin, who gave a disgruntled nod and raised his staff again, the shadows jumping back to life.

"Let's . . . have a chat about this later," Rosa whispered to the others. "I agree that he's . . . not quite what I was expecting, but then I think he is perhaps very true to the myths. I suppose wizards from the Middle Ages are going to have slightly different . . . perspectives from us."

"I'll say," said Tilly, feeling rather mutinous.

"Have you finished chattering?" Merlin asked. "Let us proceed. As I said . . . Igraine was with child, but I had Uther swear to me that the payment for my help was that their firstborn child would be given to me and left under my protection."

At this, the shadows formed into the familiar outline of a man in billowing robes clutching to his chest a bundle of blankets as he ran. The cry of a baby seemed to echo through the cave. The scene morphed into the baby being handed to a shadow man and woman, who took it carefully in their arms.

"The child was Arthur, the once and future king, as say the myths. And so he was raised in secret, with none but Sir Ector and his good lady wife, Lady Margery, knowing the true identity of the baby delivered to them. Even their own son, Kay, believed the boy to be his brother."

"But what does all this have to do with *The Book of*

*Books*—the important bit?" Alessia asked impatiently. "It's all very dramatic, but we're actually in a bit of a rush."

Merlin let the shadows vanish and looked at them properly for the first time.

"There are more of you than I was expecting," he said after a brief contemplation. "And I find I am not quite clear who . . ." He paused and furrowed his brow before pointing his staff at Tilly. "You?" he said. "You must be the Anonymous Reader—I know you, Matilda Pages."

"Uh, no, we've never met before," Tilly insisted. "And I'm not the Anonymous Reader."

"But your blood awakened my symbol, did it not?" Merlin frowned. "And I recognize you. Was it not you who spoke when I first arrived?"

"Well, I cut myself accidentally on the rock," explained Tilly. "But I'm . . . How do you know my name?"

"I have been aware of you your whole life, child," Merlin answered. "You are from a long line of book readers and makers, but you, individually, are also a curiosity, are you not? For you are not wholly of either world, and Story has long wanted you back."

"That was your fault?" Tilly spluttered, thinking of the several times she'd had to fend off bits of books trying to drag her inside.

"Ah," said Merlin, waving his hand, "'fault' is such a crass word. Perhaps I will share more with you later—once we have dealt with the immediate matter at hand. Who is the Anonymous Reader then, if it is not Matilda Pages?"

"Me," Milo said quietly, stepping forward. Merlin looked him up and down and nodded.

"I learned from Arthur, who was a gangly, skinny thing when he was first anointed, not to be deceived by appearances, boy," Merlin said after a judgmental stare. "You may not have the stature of a warrior, but . . . What is that hanging by your side?"

Milo looked down to see the soggy wooden sword still clinging limply to his belt. He pushed it to the back sheepishly.

"Nothing," he said.

"Hmmm," replied Merlin, looking unconvinced. "And who are your companions then?"

"These are my friends Oskar and Alessia," Milo said, pointing to the two other children. "And this is Rosa, the guardian of *The Book of Books.*"

"Ah, of course, I should have known," Merlin said somewhat dismissively. "I know there is one who guards the Book from the other side of Story. I did not realize it was a woman."

"This Merlin is a lot worse than the one in the TV show," Oskar muttered under his breath.

"Anyway, I am coming to the Book," Merlin said. "Do you not know how to listen to a tale well told? For though the myths start here, with Uther and Igraine, with Arthur's birth, my story began long before then. I was the one who decided that Arthur should be the hero of that story, to better tell my own in its shadows. Because I had long seen the power that was held in the creation of stories and of legends—the way that the gathering and the telling of these tales add power to them. I needed to mold as powerful a legend as I could, one that would be told for generations and generations to come, so that I could dwell inside it eternally. I had been experimenting with the magic of story for a long time before Arthur came into existence, and I wrote the Book to ensure the secrets of bookwandering, as I came to call it, would never be lost."

"So you wrote the Book yourself?" Rosa asked.

"I did," said Merlin. "I was the first bookwanderer, and I will be the last. As a precaution, I created a method whereby only one worthy reader in every generation would be able to access it."

"But why did you put a gateway to it in Pages & Co.?" Tilly asked.

"My experiments quickly showed that there needed to be a bridge built between here and your world that ensured the Book stayed connected to bookwanderers. The bridge is rooted here and enchanted to find purchase in your world. And it has moved around over the generations, but I have magicked it to stay connected to a family of great book magic, and it has been with your family for a long time now."

"That's why we came here," Milo interjected bravely. "Because everything's going wrong, Merlin. Do you know that someone's trying to find the Book and steal it?"

"I have sensed the shifts in imagination," Merlin said,

gracefully climbing down from the rock and coming to stand closer to the group. "I have felt the pressures on its limits and its boundaries. But fear not, the Book cannot be stolen. The only people who could find it and read from its pages are standing here."

"Not that I doubt that," Rosa said carefully, "but is there any chance we could just check the Book is okay, and maybe have a quick chat about how best to keep it safe going forward? We know that the man who's hunting it will do anything to access it, and he's keeping Tilly's family prisoner as we speak, to try and force us into helping him."

"It is interesting, is it not?" said Merlin, ignoring Rosa's question. "The Anonymous Reader and a descendant of the Pages family have found their way to me together. Why, it makes for a very neat story."

"It won't be if we don't make sure the Book and my family are safe," Tilly said.

"Very well," Merlin said. "Let us go to the Book."

"Is it here at Tintagel?" asked Milo.

"No," Merlin said. "We must travel to London for that, to the great church of that city. I wonder, would you like to see a boy fulfill his destiny?"

Oskar's eyes lit up. "You mean we're going to . . . ?"

"Aye." Merlin smiled for the first time. "To see the sword be pulled from the stone."

 **6**

## On the Cusp of a Story

**M**erlin led them out of the cave and back to the beach, where a completely different scene lay before them in the frosty early-morning light. There was no shiny bridge, no visitor center, and no handrails for the crudely cut stone steps they had to negotiate to get back up onto the headland. The headland itself was restored a little; great chunks of it had not yet crumbled into the sea. Everyone except for Merlin was very out of breath when they reached the top. And, of course, gone were the helpful signs and the guides and the ruins from all different ages—now there stood only a grand castle, just like the one in the cave shadows.

"Have we gone back in time?" asked Oskar, staring up at the fluttering flags.

"No, we've gone back in Story," said Merlin.

"The wrong layer!" Alessia whispered. "Just like Rosa said, we arrived in the wrong layer to start with."

"So . . . are we inside a book?" Tilly asked, trying to work it out. She knew what the expanse of Story was like, but this wasn't that; this was a place and a time and a specific tale.

"We are on the cusp of a story," Merlin answered. "Book-wandering, the ability to travel within a story, existed long before the printed book as you know it. I helped shape rules to guide the magic in a world of the written word, but the magic of imagination does not need to be bound into pages, although that medium can certainly help it along."

"That's what your father's trying to master, right?" Milo said under his breath to Alessia, who nodded. "A way to use all that power without printed books?"

"It seems like the final things he requires are indeed in Merlin's Book then," she replied quietly. "It's even more vital that we keep it out of his hands. It sounds like it contains everything he needs to help him control all imagination across the world."

Milo shivered at the idea.

Merlin gestured for them to gather round and form a circle, with Rosa gripping Merlin's staff to complete the chain. Milo, who was on the other side of the wizard, was almost surprised to find that he could touch Merlin. Milo didn't think he would have been shocked if his hand had gone right through Merlin's robes.

Merlin closed his eyes, and Tintagel click-clacked down around them, the sea and the castle dissolving under their feet to reveal a London that was nothing like the London that Tilly and Oskar knew, except for the bustle of all different kinds of people.

"What time is this?" Alessia asked curiously.

"We are out of time," Merlin answered. "This London was never real in the way that you understand it. It exists in the stories that take place here, and does not always correspond with how history might have unfolded as you were taught."

"I'm not sure if Merlin is real in any way I understand either," Oskar whispered to Milo.

"One thing I've learned from all of this," he replied, "is that my previous idea of 'real' is not especially useful anymore."

Oskar laughed.

They were standing outside a grand church, the most impressive building in sight. A crowd of men, some in clanking armor and some in extravagant church robes, were gathered in the courtyard, all focused on the same thing. People parted to let Merlin pass without seeming to even realize what they were doing, allowing the others to easily follow in his wake. Even as they stood at the very front of the crowd, no one acknowledged their presence.

"I do not want them to see us," explained Merlin before anyone had even asked the question. "It serves no purpose to have to answer to their clamoring, and I simply want you to watch for now."

A man robed in white with a heavy gold cross around his neck quieted the crowd from a raised platform.

"I spoke to Merlin," he called in a deep voice, "and he advised that I summon you, knights and lords, for, since the death of King Uther Pendragon, we have had no sovereign to lead us and protect us, and there is no heir. So here lies the sword in the anvil . . ."

The bookwanderers were immediately distracted.

"There's no stone?!" Alessia said, affronted. "Why is there no stone!"

"Pay attention, girl," Merlin said. "Look, the anvil rests on a mighty stone, and see what is carved into it."

Indeed, the great iron anvil rested on top of a huge block of marble, and on its side, written in capital letters of gold, were the words: WHOSO PULLETH OUT THIS SWORD FROM THIS STONE AND ANVIL IS RIGHTWISE KING TRUEBORN OF ALL ENGLAND.

While the others were overwhelmed by awe and wonder, Milo could only focus on the fact that presumably, in the very near future, he was going to be required to do something to prove that he truly was the Anonymous Reader, and, judging by Merlin's tastes, it was going to be some strange feat that he would almost definitely fail at. As he worried about this, he stuck his hands in his pockets and realized that the ring he had taken from the cave was still there.

*I must remember to give it back to Merlin*, he thought to himself.

Once the churchman had stopped speaking, several of the

knights started edging forward, hope and ambition glittering in their eyes.

Merlin sighed. "Men can never resist this sort of thing," he said. "Too many of them think deep down that they are the noblest of them all, that they would make an excellent king. It is not enough to be courageous and righteous knights, which many of them are. Indeed, several will become part of Arthur's Round Table, like Lancelot here—look."

A tall and very handsome young knight stepped forward to cheers from the assembled men. He gave a slightly bashful smile before gripping the sword pommel firmly and bracing himself against the marble.

His smile turned to a grimace, and his face flushed red as he put his whole strength into the endeavor, but the sword wouldn't move at all—it was stuck fast. Lancelot tried several times, but eventually had to admit defeat, and a succession of similarly tall and dashing knights met the same fate. Merlin, hidden from them all, guffawed as he watched, and would not have looked amiss with a bucket of popcorn in his hand.

"Ah, a good idea on my part," he chortled to the bookwanderers. "Never fails to tickle me. But there we are—enough of that. Come, form the circle again, friends."

Another flash of bookwandering magic emanated from Merlin's staff, and the knights and churchmen melted away, leaving them standing in a now empty and peaceful courtyard.

"It's so quiet," Tilly breathed. There was no bustle and noise from in or outside the church.

"They are all at the joust," explained Merlin. "For it is New Year's Day, and a great celebration is being held outside the city walls. Sir Ector and Sir Kay are tilting, but Kay has realized that he lost his sword somewhere along the way, and his younger brother has gallantly offered to retrace their steps and find it for him. He has had no luck at their lodging house, which is now locked up as all are at the joust. And so . . ."

He stopped talking and looked at the entrance to the churchyard, where a slender teenager with strawberry-blond hair appeared, tentatively sticking his head round the gateway. Spotting the sword buried deep within the anvil, and after only a moment of uncertainty, he walked purposefully toward it.

Arthur approached the plinth just as the noonday bells started ringing from the church tower, the only sound in the deserted courtyard amid a deserted city. Tilly had witnessed a lot of magic over the last year, but the sight of Arthur taking the mythical sword in his hands gave her goose bumps nevertheless. He braced himself, as Lancelot had done, but there was no need, for the sword slipped smoothly from its holding place, as it was destined to do. A *sudden gust of wind whipped* up the leaves from the ground, and they danced in a whirlwind around Arthur, dropping back to the ground as the last bell rang out.

"Let us say hello, shall we?" Merlin said, and with a more gentle tap on the stones with his staff, the six of them became visible to the new king, who jumped at their appearance but recovered his composure quickly.

"Oh, Merlin, it is just you!" he said in relief. "Do not be angry with me. I must retrieve a sword for my brother, Kay, to spar with, and this was all I could find."

"I am not angry," said Merlin, smiling, resting a proud hand on Arthur's shoulder. "You have done what you must do. Fret not, I will only keep you a moment from bringing the sword to Kay, but my friends here were eager to greet you."

"Oh, hello," Arthur said with a neat bow. "I do not believe we have met before. Are you travelers?"

"Of a sort," said Oskar with a smile. "It's . . . it's really nice to meet you, Arthur. I'm actually quite a fan."

"A fan?" Arthur repeated in confusion.

Oskar tried again. "I mean, I like your work."

"Ah, thank you, kind sir," Arthur said politely, "although I don't know what work you speak of, for I have lived a very quiet life with my father and mother and brother, and we will return to Tintagel after the jousting."

"Can I . . . can I take a selfie?" Oskar asked awkwardly.

"A . . . ?" Arthur had no idea what Oskar was talking about, of course.

"Now, now." Rosa stepped in. "Let's not terrify the boy with technology he's never seen before and that probably won't work here. It's a big day for him, remember?"

"Can I shake your hand at least?" said Oskar.

"Of course." Arthur held out his hand. Oskar grasped it, and the boys exchanged a firm handshake and a grin.

"Cool," Oskar said to himself as he stepped back.

"I guess Arthur might be your comfort-blanket character?" Tilly whispered to him.

"I reckon so," Oskar said in delight. "I'm definitely going to bookwander back here when everything's sorted out. Maybe visit the joust and have a go at that. I reckon I could pick it up pretty quickly."

"Now, we will not detain you any longer," Merlin was saying to Arthur. "Away with you and get that sword to your brother. And, Arthur?"

"Yes, sir?" the young king replied.

"Well done, boy," Merlin said.

Arthur looked pleased but confused, for he hadn't seen the sign on the other side of the stone and did not yet know what legend had in store for him.

They watched as he untied his horse and set off toward the city walls at a gallop to help his brother.

"Now, back to the matter at hand," Merlin said, turning to look at Milo.

"Finally," Tilly said under her breath, thoughts of Pages & Co. and her family never far from her mind.

"Come with me," Merlin said to Milo, and crooked a finger at him. Milo obeyed, walking up to the now swordless plinth.

"There's no sword for me to pull out," Milo said uselessly.

"No, of course not," Merlin said impatiently. "For you are not called upon to be king of England, which I think is best for all concerned. You, apparently, are the Anonymous Reader."

Milo was looking desperately for any sign that might easily label his task, but there were no helpful clues to be found.

"The Book is also in the stone, Anonymous Reader," Merlin said. "If you can find it."

Milo looked hopelessly at Alessia, who started to walk toward him to help, but Merlin held up his staff to block her path.

"If it is he, then he needs no aid," Merlin said. "The Book will reveal itself."

Milo stared at the huge slab of marble and the iron anvil. Walking around them, he could see no obvious cracks or gaps—the only opening was the narrow sliver where the sword had been slotted. Awkwardly climbing up onto the top of the marble, he did try to stick his fingers in there just to check, in case the Book was a very tiny manuscript or some kind of scroll, but his fingers wouldn't even fit. Milo felt his cheeks flushing in embarrassment as the others watched, and tried not to look at their expressions of hope, faith, and pity from Merlin.

"I can do this," he said to himself. "I have to. For Tilly's family, and for Horatio, and for all imagination."

Closing his eyes and focusing, he tried to feel any sort of energy or pulse of magic, reaching out with his mind for any snag of imagination. But this whole place, somewhere in between layers of Story, was made of imagination, and so everything glowed with it. Leaning back on the anvil to try and sense something, he nearly fell as it started to slide.

Milo straightened up, opening his eyes. He looked at Merlin, who only raised an eyebrow. Seizing hold of the anvil,

Milo pushed with all his might, but none was needed. The anvil slid easily and smoothly along the stone, clanging down onto the courtyard and cracking the paving stones into pieces. There was a stillness in the air that felt thick and meaningful, and when Milo looked down he saw that there, under where the anvil had been, was a space carved into the marble, and inside that space was a manuscript.

# 7

## A Bit More Glamorous Than
## Is Strictly Historically Accurate

T ime seemed to stand still for a moment as Milo stared at the Book. He reached down and gathered it up carefully—it was bigger in height than a modern book, but quite slender in width.

Its crackling old paper was bound within a creaking cover of wooden boards covered with black vellum, and it bore no title on its cover. It was fastened with a metal clasp that looked as though it needed a key, but as soon as Milo touched it, the clasp clicked open. Milo very carefully opened the cover to pages and pages of elaborate handwriting, some parts illuminated with illustrations in brightly colored ink. It looked like one of the very old Bibles that he'd seen his uncle Horatio handle on board the Quip.

"Oh." He heard a gentle exhalation, full of wonder, from behind him and looked over his shoulder to see Rosa, pink-cheeked in awe, staring at the volume in his hands. "The Book . . . I have often wondered whether I'd ever get to see it for myself."

"Can you . . . can you read it?" Milo asked.

"I can," Rosa said. "Which is a happy thing for me in this moment, but perhaps some cause for concern when we think about the Alchemist. If he can read it without assistance, then he only needs you to push back the anvil and open the clasp. Or rather he needs you, but he thinks he needs Tilly. May I?" She gestured at the Book, and Milo willingly handed it over.

"Ah, ah, ah," Merlin said, waving his staff like a wagging finger. "No need for it to be passed around or studied. It is very fragile. And actually I have a little experiment I'd like to carry out. Milo, would you be so kind as to return the Book to its hiding place and stand back?"

Rosa gave Milo an uncertain glance but eventually nodded at him and passed the Book back. Once Milo had climbed down from the marble plinth, Merlin flicked his staff, and the anvil whooshed up from the ground and back into place, as if it were made of paper and glue, not solid iron.

"I'm curious to see if Matilda has any effect on the anvil, given her heritage," Merlin said. "Would you indulge an old man's curiosity?" Tilly looked at Milo to check that he was okay with this.

"Oh, of course," he said, standing back. "I bet you can move it too."

Tilly clambered up onto the plinth and studied the anvil, gave a shrug, and then put her whole weight behind it. She found herself thinking that maybe it would move, given that her bookwandering had always been a bit of an anomaly. But it did not. Without being asked, Oskar hopped up onto the plinth as well, and Alessia followed him.

"What do you think you are doing?" Merlin asked. "There is no potential whatsoever of you two nobodies having any effect at all on this—these are systems of magic more complex and ancient than you could possibly imagine."

"No harm in trying, though," said Oskar. "I'm just curious, like you are. But about different things maybe."

He and Alessia joined Tilly in pushing the anvil as hard as they could, and although it didn't move in any significant way, there was an undeniable wobble.

"Oh," Merlin said shortly. "That is not supposed to happen. I imagine it is because I did not place the anvil back on top of the stone with enough attention. Please do not think there is anything more to it than that."

As the three children climbed back down, they looked at Milo, and he gave them a grin. He had never derived any particular happiness from being chosen or special, and the thought that they might all share the magic was far more exciting to him.

"I think it best that we leave the Book there for now," Merlin said, to Rosa's obvious disappointment. "Given the danger it is in, we do not want to give this enemy you speak of a chance to simply take it from our hands."

"That does make sense," Rosa admitted.

"Anyway," Merlin added, "there has been much to distract you from the fact that you are all damp and shivering and no doubt in need of sustenance. I suggest we find you some dry clothes and some food."

It was only when Merlin pointed this out that the bookwanderers realized he was correct. The adrenaline and excitement had kept them warm enough, but with the relief at the Book being safe washing over them, they found that they were indeed cold and extremely hungry.

"Come," Merlin said. "Form the circle, and I will take us to an inn where we will be provided for."

Once they were holding hands, the church courtyard

folded down around them, and they found themselves standing in a cozy, toasty-warm room that smelled of something rich and buttery.

"This smells way better than Treasure Island did," Oskar whispered to Tilly.

"I guess that's the benefit of being in some kind of romantic epic," Tilly said. "Everything's a bit more glamorous than is strictly historically accurate. Not that I'm complaining."

"Merlin, what have you brought me?" a woman's voice said, and from behind a bar came a smiling middle-aged woman wearing a thick woolen dress of navy blue.

"Ah, Bess!" Merlin said with real warmth in his voice. "I have some traveler friends with me. This is Milo and Matilda and . . ." He tailed off, clearly having forgotten the others' names. "Anyway, I was hoping you could provide them with fresh clothes and something to eat and drink."

"Of course I can," replied Bess. "Welcome to the Eyrie, my loves. I'm sure I have something for all of you. Come with me, you poor things. How did you get so damp?"

"It's a long story," Alessia answered. "But it's Merlin's fault."

"Ah, he does get up to all sorts of mischief, does our Merlin," said Bess, laughing. "Now, I think I should have something to fit you all—my twins are roughly the same age as you lot, there or thereabouts. Come with me upstairs."

Bess led them to the rooms over the inn, where she sized them up.

"Right, well, tell me your names to begin with," she said kindly.

As they did so, she shepherded them into a bedroom with a large and comfortable-looking double bed at its center. From a wooden dresser, she pulled out various items of linen and wool; Tilly was relieved that nothing made of real fur made its way onto the pile. Bess crossed the landing into a smaller room and brought back some other bits and pieces to add to the collection.

"Right then," she said, and started handing out outfits to the group. "This should work well enough. Boys, off you go into the twins' room across the way to get changed. I'll be downstairs catching up with Merlin if you need anything."

In their two groups, the bookwanderers set about negotiating the clothes.

"These have definitely been legend-ified too," Tilly said, holding up a cream dress with beautifully embroidered sleeves.

Rosa laughed. "What do you mean?"

"Well, I'm sure the actual Dark Ages smelled considerably worse, right? And medieval innkeepers probably didn't have quite such beautiful clothes. It's like what Merlin said about it not being the London of the true past. We're in legend, not history, and in a big courtly epic at that, so the inn smells of stew, not animal poop and sweat, and these clothes are much fancier than they should be."

"Legend-ified," Rosa repeated. "I like that very much and

think you're absolutely right. And I'm happy for all of that because aren't these clothes lovely!"

"One question," Alessia said pragmatically. "Will they vanish when we leave?"

"Oh, that's an excellent point," Rosa said. "Everyone, keep your own underwear on! Perhaps Merlin's magic will protect us from any embarrassment, though, given that he does not seem to be subject to any of the usual rules." She hung her T-shirt by the fireplace. "And let's get our own clothes dry as quickly as possible."

A few moments later, the boys rejoined them, and they all took each other in. After a brief pause, everyone burst into laughter.

"We look properly amazing," Oskar said in delight.

"I feel like a book character," Alessia said, twirling in her outfit. She had pulled out the most luxurious-looking option and was wearing a midnight-blue velvet dress with gold brocade details around the neckline and cuffs. She swooshed it satisfyingly and rummaged in a chest of drawers before finding a brocade band that she used to push her hair back.

Tilly had chosen something that seemed simpler but had actually turned out to be harder to put on: a dark green woolen skirt, which was considerably less itchy than she imagined was accurate. It had a matching laced-up bodice with two wide straps that Tilly wore over a linen shirt with loose sleeves.

Rosa had an adult-size version of Tilly's dress, in a rich

burned-umber color, and the boys were in woolen tunics in maroon and navy over warm, comfortable leggings. They all kept their own shoes on, even if they were a little damp.

"Are we . . . are we keeping our swords?" Milo said, a little embarrassed.

"I am," Oskar said, not at all embarrassed. "From a distance, it might make someone think we're armed, and you never know when you might need to trip someone up. Or push a high-up lever, or something along those lines."

That decided, the four of them strapped their wooden swords around their waists.

"Shall we head downstairs then?" Rosa said. "I know I could definitely do with a meal. And some more answers."

# 8

## I Never Said I Was a Hero

**M**erlin and Bess were waiting for them by a roaring fire.

"Ah, look at you!" Bess said, delighted. "Dressed like proper Britons instead of in those funny things you were wearing."

"I'm not British," Alessia said archly. "I am Italian."

"Oh, that sounds fancy," Bess said with a smile. "I did think your accent was a little different. Now, I don't know what they eat there, but how about I fetch you some bread and stew."

They all nodded gratefully, and a few moments later Bess and a serving girl returned with bowls full of delicious-looking beef stew packed

with potatoes and carrots, and a huge, roughly shaped loaf of bread. They eagerly dug in.

"I don't think I've eaten a proper meal since breakfast," Oskar garbled. "This is so good. Thanks, Bess."

She grinned. "You're welcome, you little charmer. I'll leave you to it. Just call if you need anything."

As soon as Bess had gone, Rosa put down her bread and looked at Merlin.

"May I ask you some questions?" she said.

Merlin nodded his agreement. "I was expecting you to."

"You said that Lady Nimue imprisoned you under the tree, and you're right—that is how I know the end of your story from the versions we have where we're from. But in those stories, and as you said yourself, she took your magic. So how do you still have, well, magic?"

"An astute question," Merlin said. "The answer is that she took the magic that she knew of, that of sorcery and spells, the magic I had taught her. She could not take what she did not understand, and even I did not truly comprehend the power of imagination, of bookwandering, back then; I had only an inkling of its potential. That strand of magic had always been tangled up with all my other powers, and it was only when they had abandoned me that I had to wrangle with what my imagination could truly achieve. It had been a blunt tool, but in my prison I was forced to sharpen it. It was then that I learned there is no stronger magic in the world, that everything is rooted in it, everything comes from it, and all other forms of magic flow from it."

"And *The Book of Books* is what you learned?" Milo asked.

"Yes," said Merlin. "My grimoire, if you will. As I discovered how to shape and use imagination, I made a record. It contains the sum of my knowledge, all it can be used for and the ways to control it, to give it, and to take it away. This is why it must be protected."

"So I'm assuming you couldn't leave the world of Story?" Tilly asked.

"Correct," Merlin said. "I created a gap in between the layers of Story, where you first found me. A gap that I widened and widened as I understood the magic more deeply. Initially, I couldn't even leave that pocket of Story, but I learned over decades and centuries how to travel within imagination and Story, so now the real world, your world, is the only place closed to me."

"But you know some things about it?" said Alessia. "Because you recognized Tilly almost straightaway."

"But not by sight," explained Merlin. "I cannot see into your world, but yes, I recognized the shape of her imagination, and the fact that she is partly of Story. Tilly exists in a similar gap to me. One she has carved out, however unintentionally, by her very nature."

"And you were the one trying to pull me into Story when we were looking for the Archive?" Tilly said accusingly, remembering his admission in the cave. "That caused a lot of problems."

"Aye, of a sort," Merlin said, nodding. "Truly, child, do not take it to heart. I could sense you; I could sense that you were a little . . . wrong, and I was curious. I wondered if I could pull you back, but I have little power in your world, so all I could do was send pulses of imagination through the pages of the books you encountered."

"That doesn't seem like a very heroic thing to do," Alessia said, raising an unimpressed eyebrow.

"I never said I was a hero," Merlin said. "I am not interested in good or bad; I exist beyond your understanding of these things. I am only interested in protecting imagination. And if I had known Matilda was a child, one who was not causing such ripples in Story on purpose, maybe I would have gone about things differently. But I was merely a curious wizard who could not see through the veil clearly. I hope you will not hold it against me, Matilda. I promise you it was not a personal slight, and I do regret if it caused you undue distress."

"Thank you," she said cautiously.

"And so onward," Merlin said, clapping his hands together. "You are satisfied the Book is safe, yes? So, what is your plan now? Will you still try to stop this enemy, even though you know it is guarded thus?"

"Yes, we must," Rosa said. "He has Tilly's family and Milo's uncle captive in Pages & Co."

"I know my father, and he won't stop until he has what he wants," Alessia added. "He will find a way here eventually."

"And who is your father?" Merlin asked. "I believe I have felt the ripples, nay, the great waves, he has been causing in imagination. But who is he and what does he want to do with the Book?"

"His name is Geronimo della Porta," Alessia answered. "And he is an alchemist, the Alchemist. He combines alchemy with his studies of book magic, and he's already gathered much of the world's knowledge for himself through hoarding books of great power. He leads a small group of bookwanderers who believe that they should control everything, but he sees the others just as tools to help him get what he wants. He has already done a lot that you have in his experiments—he works outside the normal rules much of the time, and he can travel without a book, like you can, although we believe his abilities are tied to one particular book at the moment."

"I have no doubt that he will use the information in the Book to take all the power and magic of imagination for himself," Rosa said. "To learn what you have learned, but to use it to increase his own power and influence, not for the good of others or to protect bookwandering. He will take control of every other person's imagination so they cannot use it for themselves. All will be powerless before him."

"And we also need to wake my uncle up," Milo added quietly.

"Of course," Rosa said quickly. "The Alchemist poisoned Milo's uncle, and we have almost all the ingredients we need to make a potion to cure him. It is imperative that we find a moment to do that before too long."

"So you plan to cure your uncle, Milo, and rescue your family, Matilda, before you deal with this enemy?" said Merlin. "It is the human way to do things in that order, so I will not try to convince you otherwise. What do you require for your potion?"

"I need to go and get something from *The Railway Children*," Milo answered. "It's a novel that means a lot to my uncle. And to me."

"Well, that is simple," said Merlin. "I shall send you directly from here, and that will be one task easily achieved. And I shall send Matilda with you. If this Alchemist believes her to be the Reader, it is perhaps safest not to have either of you waiting here, even briefly. Besides, you will be back in the blink of an eye."

And, before anyone had a chance to protest, Merlin reached out and touched Tilly and Milo on the shoulder, and the inn fell down around them, leaving them standing in a beautiful field in summer, with the sound of train tracks rattling behind them.

# 9 ★

## As Good a Plan as Any

**M**ilo felt slightly queasy in a way that he hadn't since he had first bookwandered and wasn't yet used to the sensation.

"Goodness," Tilly said, catching her breath, "I suppose Merlin's not used to having to work as a team, is he?"

"Definitely not," Milo said, taking a deep breath of the countryside. Being back in his comfort-blanket book brought a much-needed dose of calm and clarity amid the chaos. He breathed in fresh Yorkshire air and smiled at Tilly, for a moment almost forgetting why they had been sent here.

"So, do you know what we're looking for?" Tilly asked, bringing him back to reality. "I don't know where in the book Merlin has sent us, and surely he'd have no way of knowing if there was a particular part that Horatio liked? And . . . hang on, how do we get back?"

Milo looked at her in horror.

"Will Merlin know when we're ready?" he asked anxiously. "It seems like he can see inside Story—so maybe we just sort of shout that we want to come back?"

"I hope so," Tilly said. "I don't even know if we're in, like, a specific copy of the book, or what. He obviously doesn't have to follow the same rules we do."

"Does the Source Edition of this still exist?" Milo asked. "At the Underlibrary?"

"I don't think so," replied Tilly. "I think it would have been there when we freed them all, so there's no danger of us messing anything up in any serious way. And Merlin wouldn't have sent us here if he couldn't get us back. I'm sure of it. For one thing, it's not like Rosa would just sit there nicely and say, 'Oh well, you lost them, never mind.' And neither would Alessia or Oskar. They'll make sure he finds us one way or the other."

And the thought of Alessia insisting that Merlin find them did indeed bring Milo some comfort.

"Do you know *The Railway Children* very well?" he asked Tilly, not wanting to take charge if Tilly were as familiar with the story as he was.

"A little bit," she said. "I've only read it once, so I don't know it half as well as you do. And I've never bookwandered here—what do you think we should do?"

"I suppose we need to orient ourselves in the story." Milo thought for a minute. "So we should either try and find the children's house or go down to the railway. I can't say I recognize this particular field, so perhaps it's best to follow the sounds of trains, and I can try and find my way from there?"

Tilly nodded. "Sounds like a plan. Let's go."

It was clear from the noise that the railway line wasn't far, and they easily followed the hill downward until they found themselves by the tracks, a charming station just visible a little way off.

"Oh, we're on the other side of the tracks to normal," Milo said as they approached.

He knew that it didn't really matter that he hadn't been able to work out where they were straightaway, but he was glad there was a reason nonetheless. As they watched, the tracks started vibrating, and a whistle announced the approach of a grand steam train slowing into the station.

"Makes me miss the Quip." Milo sighed at the sight of the train. "I didn't even think about leaving her somewhere safer when we came through the portal—what happens if the Alchemist finds out she's there? He's been after her for years and years."

"For one thing, he's obsessed with the Book now it's almost in his grasp," Tilly said. "And for another, if he finds his way to the Book, he'll be coming via Pages & Co., not by the Hadrian's Wall portal, so he won't see the Quip."

"And I have the whistle," Milo reminded himself. "So I don't think he could even do anything with the Quip if he found her."

Tilly nodded reassuringly. "I get why you're worried, but I think we have a while before he refocuses his search for her. Meanwhile, look at this super-fancy train! I've never been on a non-magical steam train. Just imagine what it must be like inside!"

And, as Tilly spoke, the strangest thing happened. One moment they were standing on a grassy slope, watching the train, and the next they were sitting inside it, on blue velvet seats, the train rattling along beneath them. They exchanged an amazed look.

"How on earth did that happen?" Tilly said breathlessly.

"Did you . . ." Milo paused, trying to remember exactly what Tilly had said. "Did you say something about imagining what it would be like?"

"Yes, I think so. Is that . . . But that's impossible. That's not how bookwandering rules work."

"But Merlin doesn't follow those rules," Milo pointed out. "And he sent us here."

"I guess so," Tilly said slowly. "It must be that then. And you know, just before we first met you, when Oskar and I were lost on our way to the Archive, I managed to imagine something into reality, or at least I think that's what was happening. I forgot about it with everything that happened afterward."

No one else was on the train apart from one middle-aged man with long hair and shabby clothes sitting at the other end of the carriage. He looked very tired and nervous, but nodded

politely at them, not fazed by their medieval clothing, before returning to staring forlornly out the window.

"Oh, look!" Tilly whispered, standing and crossing over to the other side of the carriage. "A leftover ticket! Do you think that would work for the cure?"

"Maybe," Milo said. "I'm sure that part of the reason Horatio must have loved the book is because of the trains themselves— tickets sort of represent being able to go anywhere, don't they?"

"If we were trying to wake you up, what do you think we'd need?" asked Tilly.

"Definitely some red flannel knickers," Milo said with a grin.

"Excuse me?!" Tilly laughed.

"You remember! The bit where the Railway Children stop the train from crashing into the rockfall by waving the girls' red underwear. But don't worry, it's not as scandalous as it sounds. They're more like shorts that they wear under their dresses. I was actually a bit stressed the first time I bookwandered into that bit, as you can imagine, I'm sure, but they're like . . . bloomers! They're huge!"

Milo was immediately a little bit embarrassed, but it was a good feeling to make a friend laugh. He thought about how the last time he had bookwandered here, he was by himself, almost addicted to the feeling of being part of the railway family. And now here he was with a new friend, and it was even better being in the story with her. They'd have to all come back, Oskar and

Alessia too, and have tea with the family together, he decided.

"I think it's as good a plan as any," Milo said out loud, picking up the ticket. It was bent at the corner and had footprints on it. It looked very sad and forgotten.

"I have a feeling that we'll be able to take this out regardless, due to the absolutely wild levels of magic going on," Tilly said. "But is it best if I stick it in my pocket, just in case the normal rules are in operation and only I can take things out of Story?"

"Good idea," Milo said, handing the ticket over to her. "And, until we work out how to get back, we may as well get off here—this is their station. We could try and grab some other options?"

"Great," Tilly said, standing up as the train slowed to a halt and a guard came to open the heavy doors. The melancholy man from their carriage climbed down in front of them, very delicately, and stood uncertainly on the platform.

"Oh, it is lovely," Tilly said, looking around at the charming little station. "Isn't it! We must come back here afterward."

"We talk a lot about afterward," Milo said. "I hope there is one."

"There has to be," replied Tilly firmly. "I refuse to accept a world without stories, or one where everyone is under the control of some kind of imagination dictator, so we'll work out a way to stop the Alchemist. We just have to."

Once its passengers had disembarked, the train started quickly grumbling back to life. As the doors clanged shut, the shabby-looking man started to fret, rushing to the ticket office in a panic. It wasn't something Milo had seen before, although it felt somehow familiar. But there wasn't time to stay and watch, and while they were waiting for Merlin to bring them back, he was struck with the temptation to take Tilly to meet the Railway Children.

"Their house is just up that way," he said, pointing to the hill. "It might be a good place to look for a backup option."

Tilly nodded her agreement and turned to set off enthusiastically up the hill just as Milo was distracted by the sounds of a kerfuffle behind him on the platform. The passengers hadn't dispersed, even though the train had left, and a crowd had gathered, shouting and pointing.

"Hang on," he said to Tilly without turning, his eyes focused on the platform. "I can't place where I am in the book, but there's something happening. I feel like I should know what it is, but I haven't got anything to orient me," he muttered in frustration.

Milo took a few steps closer and realized that the crowd had formed around the tired man they had shared a carriage with. He moved closer to listen.

"If you ask me, I should say it was a police case," a young man called.

"Not it," another disagreed. "The infirmary, more like."

"Now then, now then," a loud voice filled with authority said, "I'll attend to this, if you please." It was the stationmaster, a character very familiar to Milo, but it was only when he saw the three Railway Children pelting down the hill from the other side of the station that he realized what scene they were in.

"What's that he's saying?" a farmer asked.

"Sounds like French to me," the stationmaster said (who had been to Boulogne for the day once).

"It isn't French!" cried Peter, the middle sibling of the Railway Children, as he arrived on the platform, out of breath.

"What is it then?" asked someone in the crowd as Peter pushed through to the middle.

"I don't know what it is," Peter said, "but it isn't French—I know that."

"Try him with French if you know so much about it," insisted the farmer.

"*Parlez-vous français?*" Peter asked a little awkwardly, and at that the man jerked forward, holding Peter's hands tightly and speaking in rapid French.

"There!" Peter said, always pleased to be right. "That's French. He was speaking something else before."

"What does he say?" someone in the crowd shouted.

"I don't know," Peter answered, clearly wishing he could be the hero of the hour.

"Here, you move on, if you please," the stationmaster was saying with a kind but firm hand to Peter's elbow. "I'll deal with this case."

Milo was now close enough to hear Bobbie, the eldest, who spoke much more quietly than Peter.

"Take him into your room," she was saying to the stationmaster. "Mother can talk French, and she'll be here by the next train."

The stationmaster gave a nod to Bobbie and gently took the man's arm. He flinched, clearly terrified. Bobbie screwed up her eyes in concentration and managed to pull some rusty French to the top of her brain.

"*Vous attendre*," she said slowly. "*Ma mère parlez français. Nous . . .*"

But the rest faded, and Milo's ears started ringing in panic as it all slotted into place. For this was the Russian writer who was fleeing prison for writing stories that got him into trouble, and part of the problem was that he had no English and no train ticket . . . It must have been Russian he had been speaking before.

"Sir, sir!" he called, trying to push through the crowd, but they were all focused on Bobbie and the man, who were walking hand in hand toward the stationmaster's office.

Milo felt in his pocket for the ticket, but of course he had given it to Tilly. "Tilly, I need that ticket back!" he said, whirling round, but to his dismay, Tilly was on her way up the hill. "Tilly!" he yelled, and she turned, surprised to see him so far behind her. "I need the ticket—I need to help!"

Tilly looked confused but immediately started back down the hill toward him. But before she reached him, there was a pulse and a sweet smell on the air, and Milo felt the familiar tug around his belly button as the bookwandering magic kicked in.

# 10

## These Things Matter in Stories

How did you do that?" Milo asked as the walls of the inn emerged around them.

"Do what?" Merlin said, leaning nonchalantly against the fireplace.

"Bring us back!"

"Oh, that wasn't me," he said with a smirk. "Although I could have, of course. I was going to give you a little more time to find whatever you needed. It was Matilda who brought you back."

"Huh?" said Milo, turning to Tilly in confusion. "Why?"

"I thought you were shouting for help!" Tilly said a little bashfully. "And so I imagined that we were back here—I honestly didn't think it would work, but I thought it was worth a shot if we needed to get out of there!"

Merlin smiled. "Matilda, you are a quick student indeed. And clearly well attuned to the power of this place."

"I did need help, but not for me," Milo explained. "For the Russian man. The ticket we picked up—it was his. And in the book, part of the problem is that he's lost his ticket. I just wanted to help."

"But . . . if he's lost his ticket in the book, then that's what always happens, right?" Oskar said gently.

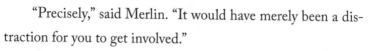

"Precisely," said Merlin. "It would have merely been a distraction for you to get involved."

"I know that," Milo said quietly. "It doesn't mean I didn't want to help."

"Do not distress yourself, child," Merlin went on. "If the man lost his ticket in the book, you know that he will always have lost his ticket, for it is how it is written. It is inevitable."

"But how does that work with Source Editions?" Alessia asked. "The ones that were left after Tilly freed so many of them? Because you can change things in those—and my father is using one to channel his powers. Have Source Editions always existed?"

"You already know the answer to that," chided Merlin. "Imagination predates the written word, and it predates printed books by a long way. I used to be able to sense much more of what the Underlibraries were doing, but over time they have cloaked themselves somehow, kept themselves more hidden from everyone. Created more rules—and people do love to follow rules. Once a group of people are told that something is true and important, it does not take very long at all for that to be absorbed as reality."

"Why?" asked Milo.

"The usual reasons," Merlin explained. "Power, control, influence. If an institution has a very important thing to protect, then it will say that it cannot be questioned, and challenging it becomes hard. But I felt a shift recently—you said this was Matilda's doing? Alessia said that you freed the Sources? You worked out for yourself that they did not need to be bound like that? I am impressed."

"I didn't do it by myself," Tilly said. "Milo and Oskar helped a lot; we did it as a team. With Horatio, who we need to wake up."

"You found what you needed then?" asked Rosa. "In *The Railway Children*?"

"I think so," Tilly replied, and pulled the bent ticket from her pocket. "We're not sure if this will work, but it was what we could find."

"Hopefully, any token from a reader's formative book will work," Rosa said. "Merlin, is there somewhere I could set up my equipment to try and create this cure?"

"You can do it here," Merlin said, giving his staff a tap, and the other customers were gone, as was Bess. "You say Horatio is also trapped in Pages & Co.?"

"Yes," Milo said. "We need to get the cure to him."

"I propose that's exactly what we do then," Merlin replied. "We will return to Pages & Co."

"So, are we in the book that's in Pages & Co.?" Tilly said.

"Not quite," answered Merlin. "As I said, the book in your family's bookshop is a gateway—another portal like the one you arrived through. In fact, the only other one. I needed to maintain that link with your world to ensure the Book's powers were intact—that its protections were working on bookwanderers. If there was only one, it would be too risky. The one in your bookshop is a precautionary measure."

"I can't believe there's a whole portal hidden in Pages & Co. that none of us ever knew about," Tilly said. "Where is it?"

"Let us go and find out," said Merlin. "It moves when it needs to so that it remains in a place of great book magic. Therefore, I do not know exactly where it will be hidden. But I do not think we should all go. If your families are being held prisoner, then their safety is, of course, of utmost importance, and it seems unlikely that six of us will be able to find a way in and get the requisite people out without being noticed if this Alchemist is as powerful as you say."

"I agree," Rosa said. "And I don't want any of you putting yourselves in any more danger than needed. I will go with Merlin, and you should wait here."

"Surely you know I'm coming too," said Tilly.

Rosa sighed, obviously expecting this response. "Okay, Tilly, I will not try to stop you, but the rest of you must wait here and get my kit set up and our ingredients ready. They are all in my backpack upstairs in Bess's room."

Oskar stood up. "I'm obviously coming too," he said, "if Tilly is."

"It's too dangerous," said Tilly. "I need you to stay safe in case something goes wrong."

"And I won't be entering Pages & Co. myself," said Merlin. "Remember, I cannot travel into your world. I shall guard the gateway and ensure your return. But I will offer you these." He pulled two triskele symbols on cords from inside his robes and gave one to Milo and one to Tilly. "These are connected. Milo, you will remain in Story and should pay attention to what Matilda has learned—that there are no limits to your imagination. Matilda, if you can get inside any book or story, this symbol will bring you here to its sibling. It will not work from your world, I do not think, for while your powers stretch across the realms, mine do not."

"But it's my uncle," Milo said. "I should go too."

"And it's my father!" Alessia said, hands on her hips.

"Alessia, I need you here getting the cure ready," Rosa said firmly. "You have seen enough of my work, and collected the ingredients, and know your father's mind—you should stay and be in charge of the recipe." Alessia glowed with pleasure at the compliment. "And we cannot all simply march in. We will be too conspicuous, as Merlin says. We need to ensure we do not all get trapped at the Alchemist's mercy if our rescue attempt fails. I don't want to give orders, but I think Tilly and I should go, even just to scout out what the situation is. We have access to this portal as many times as we require, remember, and if we need backup, we can always come and get you. And Milo should stay, as the Anonymous Reader, should he need to take the Book and run. Not that it will come to that, I'm sure." Milo did not believe Rosa's attempt at a reassuring nod.

"That makes sense," Oskar said begrudgingly. "As long as you don't do anything dangerous, Tilly. Even if you see your family, just get a look at what's what, okay?"

"That's very sensible for you," said Tilly, trying to joke.

"I can't lose my best friend," Oskar said simply. "Not to mention the fact that my mum would be so angry if I got stuck in Arthurian legend forever. She's only just wrapped her head round the whole bookwandering concept."

Tilly gave Oskar a huge hug and then nodded at Rosa. "Let's go."

"Us too," Alessia said, and they divided into their two teams of three and got to work.

As Milo, Alessia, and Oskar made their way upstairs to assemble the ingredients for the cure, Tilly and Rosa followed Merlin out the door of the inn. As they passed its threshold, there was *suddenly* a shimmer across the air, and instead of **standing** in front of the inn, they found themselves at the foot of an ancient tree.

"This is the portal?" Tilly asked, looking up at the gnarled branches.

"Aye," Merlin said, and gestured at a point on the bark. There, on the trunk, was a carving of Merlin's symbol, and at a touch of his staff it glowed, as if lit from within the tree. As Tilly watched, the glowing line spread from the triskele,

creeping across the trunk to form the outline of a door, Merlin's symbol as its handle. Then, with a click and a creak, the door swung open to reveal cavernous darkness.

"I don't mean to sound paranoid," Tilly said, peering nervously into the gloom, "but didn't you just tell us that you were tricked and imprisoned under a tree?"

"I did," said Merlin. "But that was a hawthorn tree, a symbol of magical enchantment, and this is an elm, the symbol of wisdom and life." He said it matter-of-factly, as though they could have no possible follow-up questions, and indeed, when Tilly glanced at Rosa, she seemed a little comforted.

"These things matter in stories," she said, and if it was good enough for Rosa, it was good enough for Tilly.

"I have to remain here at the threshold," Merlin said, pulling the door open more widely. "But you will find a book on the other side, a physical book, a book of the legends of Merlin and Arthur, and if you read yourself into that, you will find yourself back here. I created that book as a doorway. It is the only one of its kind and can take you nowhere but back to this tree, where I will be waiting with the door open. And you have your triskele if you need an alternative route."

And with that, Tilly felt Rosa take her hand, and they stepped

into the

**darkness** together.

# 11

## The Steps up the Chimney

After a few steps, Tilly and Rosa felt the sandy texture under their feet harden, and the air around them changed. They were standing in a small and dark space, and the earthy, damp scent of the tree had changed to something smoky and flowery.

"We're somewhere in Pages & Co.!" Tilly whispered, barely holding back her tears of relief. "I can feel it. And our medieval clothes haven't vanished, thank goodness."

"Truly, thank goodness for small mercies," Rosa said, and Tilly could hear the smile in her voice. "But where are we exactly?" That Tilly did not know.

They felt around in the darkness. Wherever they were was very small and cramped and dark, and they could not risk lighting a phone flashlight before they knew no one would see.

"Oh, there's a door here," Tilly said quietly. "A metal one, I think."

It was cold to her touch, and she could feel the ring of a door handle. She held her breath and opened it, just a crack, to let a faint light in. It was enough to see they were standing in a space that could barely be called a room, more a cubbyhole with stone walls and a stone floor. Tilly peeked her head out the door and saw that the light seemed to somehow be coming from both above and below them. She peered upward and then downward toward it and nearly yelped out loud as she worked it out.

"We're in the chimney!" she squeaked to Rosa.

"Is the fire lit?!" Rosa asked in horror.

"No, luckily," Tilly said. "We do light it in the winter—thank goodness we're too early. It's full of flowers in the spring and summer. But how on earth do we get down? We're closer to the top than the bottom."

Rosa joined her at the doorway and looked up to see the circle of early-evening light above them and a glow from a few floors beneath coming from the shop.

"Hang on," she said, kneeling down and peering into the dingy light, then reaching out. "I think there are steps here, built into the wall."

"Steps up the chimney?" Tilly breathed in wonder. "All this time! Are they safe?"

"I guess there's only one way to find out," Rosa replied. "But first we need to find the book that'll get us back to Merlin and the others so we have an escape route."

With the door open, there was just enough light to see the

tiny room that had been built into the walls of Pages & Co. a very long time ago. There was only just enough space for the two of them, despite it being empty.

"It's a good job we didn't all come," Rosa pointed out as they searched for clues.

"If I've learned anything in the last year," Tilly sighed, "it's that bookwanderers love a symbol—I bet there's a triskele or something scratched in here somewhere."

"You are almost definitely right," agreed Rosa as they started to scour the bricks.

Sure enough, on one at about the height of Tilly's shoulders, there was a scratching of a swirled triskele that glowed softly. With a gentle jiggle, the brick was easily shaken loose, then together they slid it as quietly as they could out of its space. In the gap was a book. The space itself had been lined with thin sheets of a substance Tilly couldn't identify, keeping the book cool and safe and in excellent condition, despite its obvious age. For a secret book that so few would ever set eyes on, it was particularly lovely: a large hardback bound in maroon leather. The cover displayed only a gilded depiction of Excalibur, Arthur's sword, and no title or author. Tilly opened it gently to see pages written in the same elegant but old-fashioned hand as *The Book of Books*—Merlin's handwriting.

"Well, at least we have our way back," Tilly said. "Do we take this with us? So we don't have to rush back up those steps to get out?"

"I am nervous about taking the very thing that the Alchemist is looking for right to him," Rosa said. "I suggest we descend extremely carefully and quietly and see what we can, with a view to reporting back before we take any action."

"Hmm," Tilly said quietly. "Well, let's see what's what. I agree on that."

"Tilly, we must be careful," Rosa insisted. "We must act sensibly and calmly. But if we are able to see any of your family and can signal to them without putting you or them in danger, we will, of course, try to communicate with them—but just to show them that we know where they are and that we're working on getting them out."

"Let's go then," Tilly said, carefully laying the book on the ground, open at the sword in the stone scene. "I have some experience at speedy exits from books," she said to Rosa.

"I'll lead the way," Rosa whispered. "In case these steps are not secure. Go very carefully and quietly, Tilly. It is of vital importance."

Tilly nodded her understanding, and the two of them set off down the narrow steps inside the chimney. Only one foot fit on each step at a time, and they curved precariously round, so Tilly kept having to fight off dizziness. Thankfully, their shoes made very little noise, and it being later in the summer, there was only smoky dirt to contend with as they steadied themselves on the wall. Once they neared the bottom, the sound of voices started to echo up the chimney. Rosa turned to Tilly and put a finger to her lips.

"Would anyone like a cup of tea?" was the first thing they heard, and Tilly wasn't sure whether to laugh or cry; even in such dire circumstances, her grandma was still making sure everyone was comfortable. "If you'd just untie my wrists, I can make everyone a sandwich perhaps?"

And then Tilly realized that her family were proper prisoners, not just inside the magical dome the Alchemist had created around Pages & Co., but restricted even inside it. She felt Rosa's hand on her arm as she fought the urge to barrel down the last few steps and give the Alchemist a piece of her mind.

"Oh no you don't," came his cold voice. "No one moves without my say-so. I won't have you contacting any of your friends at the Underlibrary. Unless you would like to speak to Matilda, you will remain here while I search for the Book. And, while I am keen to have this all resolved quickly, I assure you I have all the time in the world, should it be required. If you happen to remember any useful information, it would be gratefully received."

"Actually, there is one thing," said another voice. Grandad. Tilly's heart felt like a bruise that was being pushed.

"Yes?" the Alchemist said.

"There's one book that I've always thought looked strange, and has never been bought," Grandad said.

"And that book is . . . ?"

"The title will come to me—give me one

moment," Archie went on. "It's by a Russian—Dostoyevsky, I think. *The . . . The . . .*"

"*The Idiot*," the Alchemist said with ice in his voice.

"You said it, not me," Archie replied, equally frosty.

"I warn you, Mr. Pages," the Alchemist said, "your jokes are childish and irksome, and if they continue, I will have to resort to methods of keeping you quiet that will be far more unpleasant for you than for me. You are here, and alive, because I need your granddaughter, and that is all. I advise you to remember that."

"Tilly will find a way to thwart you," Bea said. "She always finds a way."

Tilly felt a tear start to roll down her cheek at the sound of her mother's voice and was glad of Rosa's tight hold on her arm.

"Now, I will be—" The Alchemist stopped suddenly, but they couldn't see why. "I feel something," he said. "High up—on the top floors."

They heard sharp, quick footsteps up the bookshop's main staircase, and Rosa started to creep downward. The steps ended about three meters above the flowers in the fireplace, which were thankfully arranged in baskets, not glass vases. Unfortunately, they included roses. Tilly braced herself for the thorns, but Rosa stopped her from jumping down.

"We must be quiet and clever, Tilly," she reminded her. Rosa braced herself against the chimney wall and leaned down so that her head was just sticking out into the fireplace, visible to anyone in the shop.

"Archie," she whispered, but the Pages family were trying to track what the Alchemist was doing. "Archie," she repeated a little louder, but there was still no response.

"Grandad," Tilly said, leaning down as far as she could, and Archie whipped his head round, his expression a tangle of panic and hope. When he spotted their heads, he couldn't help his tears.

"My dear girl," he said. "You are amazing. What on earth are you doing here?"

Tilly found that she could not speak and Rosa took over.

"Mr. Pages, Tilly and I have a route into Pages & Co. via . . . Well, we can explain later. Are you all there and well, and are you all tied?"

"Yes," Archie hissed. "Except Horatio, who's been put on a mattress just over there. His hands are tied too, but he's not attached to anything."

He indicated with his head, and Tilly could see a very still and pale Horatio lying just behind the others. Her grandma and mum, like Grandad, were sitting on kitchen chairs, hands tied behind their backs and ankles tied to the chairs.

"Can you move at all?" Rosa asked.

"Not really," Tilly's grandma replied. "But he's gone upstairs. I don't know why—he's on at least the third floor."

"Oh no," said Tilly suddenly. "He's sensed the book. It must have had something protecting it while it was behind the symbol, but I left it out on the floor, so he can feel the imagination powering it."

"I think you're right," Rosa said. "But it will take him a while to work out where it is; I can't imagine he will try the chimney first. Let's go."

"What?" Tilly said. "I thought we were just seeing what was what."

"The plan has changed," said Rosa. "He knows there's something up there, but more importantly, your family needs our help right now, and I am not going back up those steps without them. Quickly, Tilly, down we go and let us untie them. Quietly as you can when you drop."

Tilly wanted to give Rosa a hug then and there but instead focused and lowered herself down into the flowers. Rose thorns scratched at her skin, and she felt the impact of the stone floor jangle her knees, but it barely registered. She ran to her grandad and wrapped her arms around him before urgently starting to untie his hands. Rosa was down next and went over to Elsie.

"Tilly," Grandad whispered, "I am so proud of you. We need to get Horatio out first, though—he can't fend for himself. Can we get him up the chimney?"

"I don't know," Tilly said honestly. "The strongest person would probably have to carry him, maybe loop his tied wrists over their neck? It's tight, and the steps are really small."

"Okay, then that's what we'll do," Grandad said. "Go and untie your mum, and I'll get Horatio." Tilly ran to her mum and gave her a hug as well.

"Look at you rescuing me again, you superstar," Bea said with a teary laugh. "What would we do without you, eh?"

Once they were all untied, they lifted Horatio from his mattress as quietly as they could, and there was a brief tussle over who should carry him.

"You're still weak after being poisoned," Elsie said to her husband, quiet but fierce.

"I can do it," Bea insisted, but Grandad had scooped Horatio up in his arms before anyone could stop him.

"Tilly, go first," he said. "You know where you're going and presumably how to get out. I'll come next with Horatio, and Bea can follow me in case I stumble. Elsie next, and then Rosa—if that's okay with you? I mean this with the greatest respect, but I think you're best equipped to deal with the Alchemist should anything go awry, but let us hope he stays fixated on his search, for he's certainly a single-minded man."

Rosa nodded her agreement, and Tilly could not believe that she was lucky enough to know such brave and kind people.

There was a brief, intimidating pause as they took in the challenge of actually getting back up to the steps, but with a deep breath, they started moving the kitchen chairs they had been tied to into a stack in the fireplace. Flowers were tipped from baskets so that the chairs could lie evenly on the stones, and Tilly climbed up first, the chairs making it possible to reach the first step.

Grandad, Bea, Rosa, and Elsie started manhandling

Horatio upward. It would have been awkward and difficult in any circumstances, but the necessity for speed and silence made the task feel near impossible. Although Archie said nothing, Tilly could see how pale and strained his face was as he pulled Horatio's body upward and looped his tied wrists over his neck. There was sweat dripping from his forehead, and his arms were already wobbly. But when Tilly tried to say something, he just gave her a small shake of the head.

"Onward and upward, brave girl," was all he said. "Lead the way."

Tilly started back up the steps as nimbly as she could, checking behind her to make sure Grandad was okay. Bea was right behind, hands out supporting Horatio as best she could, given the narrow steps. Elsie climbed up after her and started up the steps, but as Rosa hoisted herself up, her foot knocked against the stack of chairs, and they crashed to the floor. Everyone froze in horror, and the color drained from Rosa's face. For a moment, Tilly thought they had gotten away with it, but then there was an angry shout and the sound of running feet.

"He's coming," Grandad said. "Go, Tilly, as quick as you can."

# 12

## Surge of Imagination

In all the things that had happened in the last year, ever since Tilly had discovered she was a bookwanderer, she was not sure she had ever felt fear like it. And she had been in a truly unusual number of dangerous situations for a twelve-year-old.

"If you betray me, you will regret it for a very long time!" they heard the Alchemist bellow, his rage displacing his usual chilly composure. "Or, I should say, for a very short time!"

With her small feet and familiarity with the steps, Tilly found she could move quickly, but her grandad was struggling, and there was no way for anyone to help carry Horatio on the precarious steps. She let Grandad lean on her shoulders for a beat, but there was no time to rest, and Grandad had to keep moving, one step at a time.

"Where the devil are you?" came the Alchemist's voice, and then he noticed the fallen chairs in the fireplace. "What in the hell are you doing up there?" he shouted. "Do you think you can hide from me in a chimney like a family of mice? How pitiful!"

And then there he was. Standing in the fireplace, staring up at them in bewilderment. Tilly hadn't seen him since they had fled from his laboratory in Venice with Alessia in tow, and she had forgotten his face and the venom and the veneer of elegance it hid behind. Then he saw her.

"You," he breathed. He started to laugh. "Imagine coming back here, right into the lion's den. I knew the threat to your family's safety would lure you back, and I'm not even surprised you found a way in past my protections. But who are . . . you?" He stared at Rosa, the lowest down the stairs, realization creeping over his face with delight. "No, do not tell me you have both delivered yourselves to me. Truly, you are like mice caught in a trap."

None of them had stopped climbing as the Alchemist spoke, and Tilly was nearly at the door in the chimney now, but Grandad lagged behind still.

"Where on earth do you think you are going?" the Alchemist taunted. "You will escape over the roofs of London— is that what you think? I assure you, my boundary goes much higher than you can."

As Tilly reached the metal door, she realized that there was no way of getting back to Merlin without alerting the Alchemist to the book—and it would have taken a much less clever man than him to work out where it led. She would have to hope that she could make it work like a regular book, that it would come with them when they traveled. Swinging the door open, she heard the shout of frustration from the Alchemist as he realized something was hidden up there, that they had a plan beyond his understanding.

"What is . . . ? Oh, I see. You have come from where I felt the surge of imagination and magic. That is where it was hidden. I cannot thank you enough for showing me, Matilda. Think of all the time that you've saved me!"

And then he quickly started righting the fallen chairs and climbing up after them. He moved speedily and smoothly, as though the uneven steps were a great wide walkway.

"Go, Dad, go!" Bea cried in desperation. Tilly had the book ready; she just needed to be touching the others.

"Everyone link hands!" Tilly yelled. "Rosa, shout when you're touching Mum, and I'll read us out." She ran back down the top few stairs to meet her grandad, who had propped Horatio against the wall, holding him there with his arm, breathing heavily.

"Make sure you get Horatio to safety," Grandad said, gesturing for Tilly to hold on to him, while he took his other arm. "We need him awake, I think, for this last fight."

"We're all going," Tilly insisted, leaning over to make sure everyone was touching. "And then came Merlin!" she shouted. "The greatest magician that had been known in all . . ." And the bricks of the chimney started to clatter down and dissolve, just like in bookwandering.

But before the inside of the tree could reappear, Tilly felt an almighty tug and looked down in horror to see that the Alchemist had grabbed Rosa's ankle and was holding on. Rosa was trying to let go of Bea so that the Alchemist would not be brought along, but Bea would not let go, and Elsie refused to let go of her daughter. And Grandad, of course, would not let go of Elsie.

"Get Horatio to safety, Tilly," he said, releasing Horatio as they were tugged downward. "You can do this; I believe in you."

And with that, Pages & Co. dissolved away, taking her family with it, leaving Tilly alone with a sleeping Horatio.

# 13

## A Pretty Good Story to Be Part Of

Tilly found herself at the base of the ancient elm tree, Horatio slumped on the ground at her side. She lay stunned and exhausted for a second before realizing that she didn't have the gateway book in her hands; it had stayed put at Pages & Co. Whether through her own error or the design of the magic, she wasn't sure. A hopeful, quiet voice told her that meant that her family could still come through, but a louder, braver one reminded her that it also meant the Alchemist could too, and her grandad was counting on her.

"Merlin!" she shouted, and he was instantly there.

"Can you close the gateway somehow?" she said. "Things didn't go to plan, as you can probably tell, and we need to make sure the Alchemist can't get here—he knows where the portal is now. Can you lock it from this side?"

"Of course," Merlin said, touching his staff to the triskele door handle on the tree trunk.

The outline of the doorway dissolved back into the bark, and the tree . . . Well, the only way Tilly could describe it would be to say it ungrew. It reversed back through its aging and growing until it was a sapling, then a shoot, and then it disappeared back into the earth, leaving only dusty ground and a single forgotten leaf.

"What will happen if they try to read the book now?" Tilly asked, thinking of her family and Rosa. "They won't get stuck anywhere underground, will they?"

"No," Merlin assured her. "It will do nothing. It will be as if they are reading a normal book, or rather even more normal than usual, as there is no way to bookwander inside it, even in the traditional sense. The portal cannot be opened until I allow it."

"Okay," Tilly said, and she felt a great wave of relief and exhaustion and disappointment wash over her. Her next thought was that she needed to speak to her friends, Oskar in particular.

Merlin, displaying a little more empathy than Tilly had previously witnessed, put his hand gently on her shoulder, and with a tap of his staff, they were back at the Eyrie.

They landed hard on the stone floor of the inn due to having to support Horatio's unconscious weight, and the thump was enough to bring the others hurtling downstairs.

"Are you okay?" Oskar said, staring at Tilly with worry written all over his face.

"Where's Rosa?" Alessia added, and Milo didn't say anything, just stared at his uncle. Tilly burst into tears.

"Can we have a moment to ourselves?" Oskar asked Merlin,

who hesitated, but nodded and retreated. The other three wrapped Tilly up in a huge hug and gave her a moment to cry without asking her any questions at all.

"Everyone's still alive," she said quietly as she calmed down. "It was all going so well to start with, but the Alchemist heard us trying to escape, and we couldn't all get out in time. Grandad made me take Horatio first so he could help us, but my family are still trapped, and now the Alchemist's got Rosa as well. And he knows how to get here too, although Merlin's locked the gateway. But we'll have to open it at some point to get the others out or when we work out what to do about the Alchemist generally. Not to mention that we're still no closer to finding out how to stop him."

"And now we've swapped an awake, helpful adult for an unconscious, morally dubious one," Alessia said thoughtfully. Milo gave her a "not the time" look. "Sorry, just assessing the situation," she said a little bashfully. "I truly can't imagine how hard that must have been for you, Tilly." Tilly gave her a small, appreciative smile.

"How did you get on with the cure?" Tilly asked.

"Well . . ." Oskar started.

\*

HALF AN HOUR AGO . . .

\*

"Do you have the recipe?" Milo asked Alessia solemnly.

She nodded and unfolded a piece of paper from inside

her clothes. "I haven't let it leave my side," she replied. "It did get a bit damp when we were in the cave, but I know what I'm doing—I'm confident I'm ready for this."

As Alessia read through the slightly smudged recipe, Oskar fetched Rosa's backpack.

"Heck, this is heavy," he said as he picked it up. "Rosa was carrying this around the whole time?"

"She knows what she's doing," Milo said, finding that he felt quite proud to be able to tell Oskar about Rosa. "She takes it into all sorts of places so she can learn about botany and imagination. I hope you get to see her greenhouse at some point."

Oskar helped Milo carefully unpack Rosa's botanist's kit backpack. It was ingeniously organized, with the glass bottles and equipment safely stowed into cushioned compartments to keep them protected.

"All these things are the ingredients we gathered," Milo explained to Oskar as they arranged the bottles. "They've been turned into pure imagination so we could take them out of the books. Okay, read off the list, Alessia," Milo said. "And I'll line them up."

"First up, we need death made into life, so the twig from *The Secret Garden*," said Alessia. Milo searched the labeled bottles and pulled out the correct one, setting it carefully on the wooden floor.

"Second is a token of unnatural nature," and Milo found

the bottle that was labeled "Tumtum tree" that they had brought from "Jabberwocky."

Then came the golden arrow from the Robin Hood stories for something stolen honestly, and the runcible spoon from "The Owl and the Pussy-cat" for an impossibility. There was a twist of ginger, as the recipe stated, and then the other two more unpredictable ingredients—something lost properly, and the Record of the reader. The Lost Properly Office was a secretive department at the British Underlibrary, which gave the memories of bookwanderers who had passed away somewhere to exist and be remembered; they took on different smells and shapes and colors.

As the bookwanderers weren't quite sure how the memories would work in the cure, each of them had chosen one, meaning there were five options for this particular ingredient. When they had picked them out in the Underlibrary, they had gone for memories that seemed fresh and lively, clouds of colored smoke that bumped and nosed their way around their containers. But when Milo retrieved them from Rosa's backpack, they had changed.

"What does that mean?" Alessia asked. She picked one up, a little gingerly, as the memory inside was moving around so excitably that the small glass bottle was rocking on the uneven floor.

"Maybe it's because of where we are?" Milo suggested. "We're inside Story, in the gaps between imagination. Can they feel it? Like it's giving them new life?"

"I suppose that makes sense," Oskar agreed. "Things last a long time in stories—isn't that what Merlin was talking about? That he shaped all the Arthurian legends to make himself a space he could be immortal in?"

"You're right," said Alessia, nodding.

"It feels mean to put one in a cooking pot," Oskar said ruefully as he looked at the dancing colors that seemed so full of personality.

"I don't know," Milo said thoughtfully. "This seems like a pretty good story to be part of."

"But how do we even get it mixed in?" Oskar asked, looking down at his swirling bottle. "We can't tip this into the bowl of Rosa's distillation kit—it won't stay still. And the recipe says we have to distill all the ingredients down."

"But all of them already are, and arguably this is too," said Alessia. "That's how I understand it from what Rosa's taught me—maybe we should put all the other ingredients in with the memory and see what happens?"

"We do have five," Oskar pointed out. "So how about we set one free and see how it reacts? We can do the one I picked; I don't mind."

"I think that makes sense," Alessia said, and passed the one filled with vivid orange smoke to Oskar.

The bright cloud swooshed out of the bottle neck as soon as he uncorked it but dissipated almost as quickly as it had escaped. When they had been outside Story, only Milo had really been

able to pick up on more than the vaguest sense of the memories, but here, deep in the gaps between stories that Merlin had carved out, all three of them were overcome by it.

Overwhelming glee and wonder were immediately apparent, and the three of them understood instinctively that this was an early bookwandering memory—maybe even the first trip inside a book. *There was a breeze on the air,* as though the person were traveling, or flying, with a slightly *unpleasant* background sensation of travel-*sickness.* A squawk of a bird and the smell of singed . . . something was on the air, and a powerful urge to make a wish.

"That was amazing!" Alessia said in delight. "What was it?"

"I'm not sure," Milo replied. "I bet Tilly would know if we described it to her."

"And it definitely answers the question of how to combine things," Oskar said. "We'll bring together the other ingredients and add the mixture to one of these other memories without letting it escape. Then what do we do with the ticket?"

"We distill it down too, using Rosa's kit," Alessia answered, getting the small burner set up. "Everything has to be made into pure imagination—but we don't add that until we can give the cure to Horatio."

"What does this bit of the instructions mean?" Oskar said, pointing at the bottom of the recipe. "About distilling with the fifth element? What's that?"

"It's imagination," Alessia answered. "That's my father's alchemy background coming through. I think it's to do with the intent of the brewer, though, not a new ingredient. The cure requires a belief in the capacity of imagination—it's all the same thing that Merlin's been talking about: removing the limits on what we think book magic can do. Right, everyone ready? The recipe doesn't state quantities, so I'm going to use an equal amount of each ingredient we can measure and leave some in case it doesn't work the first time."

Milo thought it was amazing how confident and composed Alessia was under such pressure and in pursuit of defeating her own father. He felt lucky all over again that their paths had crossed. She pulled a small set of scales out of the pack and started to very gently shake each bottle of iridescent imagination dust out, adding an equal amount of each to an empty bottle.

"Rosa talked me through quite a few of the principles of her work," Alessia told Milo as she worked.

"When?!" Milo said in amazement. "We were barely there a day!"

"Oh, in small fragments," Alessia said casually. "But I made it my mission to remember everything she said. I want to be like her when I'm older. Investigate imagination, but for good, like Rosa, not like my father. Now, let me concentrate."

After a few moments, there was a small pile of dust in the bottle that looked unremarkable apart from a rainbow shimmer that flickered across it every few seconds. Alessia added an equal amount of ground ginger, gave it a shake, and sat back, satisfied.

"Now we need to get it into one of those memories," she said. "Which one looks the quietest?"

They surveyed the remaining four, and Rosa's was obviously the right choice. Midnight blue in color, it was swirling far more gently around its bottle than the others, which were still fizzing and darting. Alessia pulled out a small metal funnel from Rosa's kit that would fit flush into the neck of the bottle, and in one slick movement she uncorked it, inserted the funnel, tipped the mixture quickly and neatly inside, and recorked it. The whole thing took only a few seconds, and Oskar and Milo both spontaneously burst into applause. Alessia's cheeks went pink with pleasure, but she stayed focused.

The three of them watched, entranced, as she gave the bottle a very gentle swirl, and the blue smoke floating above the dust started weaving its way through the particles. There was the smell of toasted marshmallows on the air, and sparks erupted in the bottle. Alessia held it steady as it fizzed, and then all of a sudden the smoke and dust melted into a deep purple liquid.

"Has it worked?" Oskar asked tentatively.

"No way of knowing until we can test it on Horatio," Alessia said, and that was when they heard a thump from downstairs.

# 14

## Back to the Very Beginning

The four children considered but ultimately disregarded a plan to try and get Horatio up the stairs and onto Bess's bed. Instead, Milo and Alessia lifted him up onto one of the benches by the fire as Oskar sat by Tilly with a protective arm around her shoulders.

"I don't think they've invented hot chocolate yet, otherwise I'd get you one," he said, which produced the suggestion of a smile from Tilly.

"Did the memories work okay?" she asked Alessia, who explained how they'd reacted unexpectedly in Story.

"We think it's because of them being here; it sort of gives them a new lease on life," Oskar explained. "Like how, when people write books, they live on in a way, and so do the things they write about."

"If I were to write a book," said Tilly, nodding, "I would put my grandad in it, and then he would live forever. Even after he was gone and I was gone, other people would get to meet him and know him because he was in the pages of my book. It doesn't surprise me the memories can feel where we are."

Oskar gave her shoulder another squeeze.

With Horatio lying in front of them, it was time for Alessia to carefully light on fire the ticket they had taken from *The Railway Children*, perhaps the most unpredictable ingredient of them all. It burned away to shimmering dust, and with a nod to the others, Alessia uncorked the bottle and added it. They all held their breath, waiting to see what would happen. And then, just as when they'd added Archie's Record to the cure the Alchemist had made, a flash of rainbow darted across the dark liquid.

"That bodes well," Alessia said calmly as the others let out their breath. "But only one way to check." She looked up at Milo and became a friend before she was a scientist. "Are you ready?" she asked him. "A lot has happened to us all since your uncle was poisoned, and you know a lot of things you didn't know the last time you spoke to him."

"I'm ready." Milo nodded, even if he did not think he would ever be ready. "The two of us have a lot to talk about."

"Here we go then," Alessia said as she gave the bottle a last swirl and approached Horatio. Milo lifted his uncle's head up and gently opened his mouth as Alessia tipped in a few drops of the cure. There was silence, and then a splutter and an almighty cough.

"Milo?" was the first thing Horatio said as his eyes flickered open. "What have you done now?"

Milo immediately felt like all he'd learned and done and overcome in the last couple of days was undone, and he was once again the nervous little boy scared of his uncle's temper. Horatio sat up woozily, holding his head.

"Water," he croaked, and Tilly and Oskar went to find some. "What's going on? Where am I? What did you do, boy?"

"Actually, while you've been sleeping, Milo has been busy saving the world," Alessia said sharply. "He has also been to a huge amount of effort to make this cure to wake you up. So, if I were you, I would say thank you."

Horatio looked stunned and then started to laugh. "Thank you then, Milo," he said with a shrug. "Seems like me and you need to have a catch-up."

"Uh-huh," Milo said quietly. "I . . . I've been to the Treehouse Library." That seemed a good way of summing up what he knew.

"I see," Horatio said. "And how is my dear mother?"

Alessia shot Milo a panicked look, and of all the things that Milo had been worrying about once Horatio was awake, he had completely forgotten about the fact that he was going to have to be the one to break the news.

"She . . . she died," he said abruptly, not sure how to soften it. "The Alchemist killed her."

"Oh," Horatio said, and all his sarcasm slipped away. "I see.

Did he . . . kill her for any particular purpose? Or was it pure malice? I know that she, well, that she admired him far more than was wise."

"To send a message," Milo said. "Mainly. That he was serious and would harm . . . There really is a lot to catch you up on. I suppose the key facts are that, uh, well, when you were poisoned . . . Okay, no, so we got the poison cabinet, but the eitr had run out, but me and Tilly actually accidentally took it to the Alchemist. Well, not accidentally because we needed the cure, and then Alessia rescued us, and, um, we woke Archie up, oh, and the Archive got destroyed, and then Alessia and I went to find Rosa, and then I met Lina, and turns out I'm the Anonymous Reader, which was a surprise to everyone, I think, and . . . Well, I also know about the contract you made with the Alchemist and the trap you set for Tilly and all of that side of things too. And so does Tilly. But I did learn how to drive the Quip!"

He couldn't stop the pride and need for approval from seeping into his voice, despite everything, but braced himself for the inevitable dismissal.

"You did, eh?" Horatio said with a softness that Milo was unprepared to hear. "Well, that's something. We can talk about the contract too. I . . . I owe you some explanations. But you must be Alessia?" he said, nodding his head to her. "As you're the only one here I haven't met. And hello, Matilda."

Tilly raised an eyebrow at him as she and Oskar returned with a tankard of water.

"So you learned about my agreement with the Alchemist," Horatio said, and had the grace to sound embarrassed. "You may not believe me, but I swear that it was a ruse. I never intended to leave you there with him. I just needed to protect the Quip and Milo."

"I'll decide if I believe you once we've dealt with all of this," Tilly said archly.

"That's fair," Horatio said. "Now . . . where is the Alchemist? And where is the Botanist, or Rosa as you seem to be calling her nowadays?"

"They're both at Pages & Co.," Oskar replied.

"What?"

Horatio seemed entirely surprised for the first time since he'd woken up, and Tilly noted that clearly Rosa hadn't shared with him that she knew where the gateway was. Rosa and Horatio had started sharing information to try and stop the Alchemist, but Rosa knew to keep some cards close to her chest when it came to Horatio. The group tried to fill Horatio in on as much as possible but kept getting muddled as to what everyone knew.

"My last question, for the time being," Horatio said, still rubbing his head, "is where on earth are we now?"

"You're in my domain, sir," Merlin said, reappearing at the doorway.

"Thanks for having me," Horatio said, the usual sarcasm rising as he took the measure of this new person. Milo could see his uncle assessing Merlin—his magic, his nature, his weaknesses. "I suppose we should compare notes."

"I am interested primarily in protecting the Book," Merlin said sternly. "As it would seem you understand, it holds and protects the fundamental secrets of bookwandering. And with its power, I could seal off the gateway, with you all on whichever side I choose, you understand? I could cut off all links to your world, let myself live on in legend, content myself not to be involved at all, and hope no one worthy ever needs the knowledge I protect. It is only due to the pluck and bravery of these youngsters that I do not do that."

"Noted." Horatio dipped his head.

"And, Horatio," Milo said, "Rosa was sure that you had the key—something you'd learned that will tie all this together and help us actually work out how to defeat the Alchemist. Is it to do with eitr?"

"Partly, I think," Horatio said. It was such a strange and new experience for Milo to be speaking with his uncle so frankly. "Rosa and I believed that it was a substance powerful enough to separate or end the Alchemist's hold on imagination. It's a terrifying poison from the Norse myths, potentially the strongest ever to exist. As you know, we had hoped there might be some in the poison cabinet, but clearly not. So I think we shall have to go and get it ourselves. Can we bookwander from here?"

"Yes," Tilly said. "We can bookwander like the Alchemist does, just with our imaginations."

"And that's what it's all about, I reckon," Horatio said urgently. "The thing I learned that I hadn't told Rosa yet, the missing clue, I think, is that the foundations of all this lie way back in the roots of it all. Long before even the Alchemist started experimenting and extending his life. We need to go back to the very beginning."

"But we are at the very beginning," Tilly said. "Merlin is the first bookwanderer, the one who shaped imagination into bookwandering."

"We need to go back even earlier," Horatio said. "Before bookwandering. Before the rules and the shaping. Back to the source." He was rubbing his head again. "That poison really did a number on me," he said, screwing his eyes up in pain and wobbling a little on his bench. "Listen, all of you, in case something happens to me again. You need to go and find . . ." He paused again, clearly struggling to stay focused and get the words out. "Find . . . Calliope." And then he fainted.

"Oh, not again," Alessia said.

# 15

## See You in a Few Chapters

"W hat happened?" A horrified Tilly spun round to look at Merlin.

"I suppose that something has gone awry with the cure?" he said, and they all looked at Alessia.

"It worked!" she said. "He woke up!"

"We must have been almost exactly right," Milo said. "You did amazingly."

"No, it can't be the cure!" Alessia insisted. "It doesn't make sense that it would counteract a poison and then just stop working. It's a yes-or-no thing!"

"Maybe he's just . . . really tired?" suggested Oskar. "Or, I don't know, he hit his head on something while he was being moved around?"

"There's some of the mixture left," Alessia said, holding up the bottle. "Let me try again, or at least we can get him awake for another fifteen minutes or so and ask him some more questions."

The others nodded their agreement, and Alessia tipped the remaining drops into Horatio's mouth. Nothing happened.

"This doesn't make sense," Alessia said again. "If it woke him up the first time, it doesn't track that it wouldn't work again."

"Unless the whole thing has ceased to work, whether within or without the patient's body," Merlin said.

"As in, it's gone out of date," Oskar added.

"I just don't think—" Alessia started, but Tilly interrupted.

"I'm sorry, but we need to keep going for now," she said. "Once we have Rosa back, she'll be able to work out what's going wrong, but we can't waste the rest of the ingredients on another attempt without any new information. What we need to find out is who Calliope is and where she is. Do you know?" She turned to Merlin.

"If he is talking about going back to the beginning, then I can only assume that he's referring to the goddess Calliope or, as Ovid called her, the Chief of all Muses."

"The Muses?" Oskar asked.

"Sounds like we're swapping legends for myths," Tilly said. "Greek ones."

"Wasn't Ovid a Roman?" Alessia said. "I should know, as an Italian."

"Ovid was indeed Roman," Merlin said. "Yet he was fascinated by Greek mythology; his *Metamorphoses* is one of the most enduring accounts. But there are several versions of these stories, told by many voices, some of which were lost long ago. All stories are false and all are true, and they all start somewhere."

"Huh?" Oskar said.

"Calliope will tell you more," Merlin said.

"It's not just Greek or Roman myths," Milo pointed out. "If we have to go and fetch the eitr as well, we need a Norse myth for that. And Rosa seemed sure it was the best bet of somehow separating the Alchemist from his power over imagination."

"I think we should split up," Tilly said. "To get both quicker."

"That didn't go so well last time," Milo replied cautiously.

"My suggestion is that two of us go after the eitr, and two talk to Calliope," Tilly said. "Not to try and do anything individually. I know Oskar and I are a good team; we've done harder things than find a Muse. I think," she added a little nervously, trying to sound more confident than she felt.

"And Milo and I can do pretty much anything as far as I understand it," Alessia said, matching Tilly's determination. The two girls gave each other nods of understanding. "I propose Milo and I go and get the eitr," Alessia went on. "We have more experience with alchemy and Rosa's work. And you and Oskar have more experience with bookwandering and stories and how that all works, so you should search for Calliope."

"Simple as that," Tilly said, and she and Alessia shook hands.

Tilly found that she relished being around Alessia, who was so cool and calm and collected, not to mention extremely clever. She never felt like she had to explain or justify herself to Alessia but could just be herself and would be accepted as such.

"Do you know where we find eitr?" Milo asked Alessia.

"Rosa told me," she said. "Two places, I think. In one of the old Norse poems, it talks about drops of it making a giant, but the main source is from Jörmungandr."

"Please tell me that's a nice, friendly goddess," Milo said. "Or a beautiful garden."

"Not quite," Alessia said. "It's also known as the Midgard Serpent, the middle child of Loki and a giantess."

"A giantess," Milo repeated. "So . . . it's quite big?"

"Well, it—actually, I think he—grows big enough to encircle Earth," Alessia said.

"Excuse me?" Milo said, turning pale. "Is it too late to join the Greek team?"

"But we have two options," Alessia went on. "We can either try and find him when he's young, when the gods first discover he and his siblings exist, so we'd have most of the Norse gods for backup. Or we can go to the myth where Thor fishes him out of the ocean, and then we'd have Thor there to help."

"Let's definitely try the first option," Milo said. "Fishing for a giant serpent doesn't sound like a plan A."

"Fine by me," Alessia said, gathering up Rosa's things.

"Are you sure you're okay going to get the eitr?" Tilly asked Milo. "I didn't realize it was quite so . . . dangerous."

"We'll work it out," Milo said with a waver in his voice.

"I'm sure. Sounds like we might be able to get Thor onside, and he's, you know, famously strong. And you don't know what you'll find either."

"Can you help us get to these places?" Tilly asked Merlin. "They're older than you, right? Do you have manuscripts or something?"

"I could access the manuscripts, yes," Merlin answered. "But unless you are fluent in either Latin, Ancient Greek, or Old Norse, I suggest I send you to an English translation so you can speak to the appropriate people and actually understand them. You will experience whatever version of the story is there, but Calliope will always be herself, wherever you find her. Do you wish me to accompany you?"

"No, I think it's best if you stay and watch over Horatio," Tilly replied with a nod of agreement from Milo. "Make sure that the Alchemist doesn't find a way here."

"I assure you the gateway is closed," Merlin said.

"I really don't mean to be rude," Tilly replied, "but the Alchemist is the most powerful bookwanderer who's ever existed, and if anyone can work out a way to get around your lock, especially given that he knows loosely where that book leads, then it will be him."

Merlin acquiesced. "Very well. I have no great desire to battle with Jörmungandr or argue with the Muses anyway. They think very highly of themselves. Be careful what you say around them. I will remain here and guard the Book, as I have done for centuries. And I suppose I can keep an eye on Horatio at the same time."

"Thank you," said Milo sincerely. "He's my only family now, even if he is . . . who he is."

"Now, who shall I send first?" Merlin asked.

"We're ready, but I have a copy of the book we need," Alessia said, pulling a slim volume out of Rosa's bag. "Rosa was prepared. I know where we're headed; we can bookwander the old-fashioned way."

"Oh, there's no need," Merlin said. "Let me help."

Alessia shrugged. "Doesn't make any difference to me," she said. "But please ensure it's this version, okay, so we can move around if we need to."

"Of course," Merlin said. "When you're there, remember to use your imaginations."

"We will," Alessia said, hoisting Rosa's backpack onto her shoulders and grasping Milo's hand firmly. "Please send us to where the gods are finding Loki's children." She turned to Tilly and Oskar and grinned. "See you in a few chapters . . ."

# 16

## Myths Are Even Fancier Than Legends

Chilly medieval England melted away to reveal bright, warm sunshine.

"Oh my goodness, that's nice," Alessia said, stretching her arms out and soaking it in. "And, judging by the burning rainbow bridge, I would guess this is Asgard. But the gods find Loki's children in the land of giants, not in Asgard. Hang on, let me check if they bring them back here." She riffled through the copy of the book they had. "It's not very clear," she said in frustration. "I think we should bookwander forward to the right bit."

"Maybe there's a reason Merlin sent us to this point, though?" said Milo. "Should we at least try and work out where we are? Maybe they're about to set out, and we'll need their help to get the poison safely? Or there's something we need to take with us from here?"

"Perhaps," Alessia said. "I'm not sure what Merlin's deal is, though—he thinks he knows better than all of us, even though he's just been chilling in his cave for a really long time, and we're the ones who've actually been out there, battling against evil and all that. He's very . . . imperious. Is that the right word?"

"It means arrogant, doesn't it?" Milo said, and Alessia nodded. "I guess he's just not really used to talking to modern people," Milo went on. "And perhaps he wasn't expecting four children to turn up. I don't think he's that fussed about anything apart from keeping the Book safe, which is really all we need him to do. He's just had a lot of time with not much else to think about. It's no wonder he's fixated on it."

"You're right," Alessia replied. "And his ability to just imagine anything is quite useful—saves a lot of time. Let's go with it for now. We can easily read forward or backward if we need to."

The rainbow bridge, which had a shimmery, sparkling look to it, as though it were burning without flames, led away into the sky behind them. In front was a wide paved avenue lined with fruit trees laden with apples, pears, and peaches. There was a scent of something sweet and pleasant on the air, with a metallic tang to it. Talking and laughing could be heard coming from somewhere not too far away, but they saw no gods or goddesses. There wasn't much for it but to follow the avenue up to a magnificent palace built of columns of pale stone that stretched up into the sky. Its tallest turrets had wisps of pinkish clouds tangled around them, and gleaming windows reflected the sun. Everything was clean and sparkly.

"Myths are even fancier than legends," Milo whispered.

"In Arthurian legend, the past doesn't smell bad, but here they've taken it to the next level. It smells like a sweetshop."

"I guess a city of gods and goddesses was always going to be pretty impressive," Alessia said. "I wonder where they all are."

Helpfully, at that moment, a huge roar of laughter rang out from the palace, alongside the clang of goblets being toasted.

"Let's go," Alessia said, and they picked up their pace as they walked up to the palace, through enormous golden gates set between two pillars carved as majestic wolves, each with a raven perched on its shoulder. The gold of the gates themselves was intricately wrought, with a symbol of three interlocking triangles worked through it.

Once they were through the gates, they could see where the gods were gathered. A wide courtyard had a long table running down its center, piled high with an extravagant feast and many flagons of wine. Sitting on each side were the most beautiful people Milo had ever seen. Lustrous hair was twisted into elaborate braids, thick linen robes fell in luxurious folds, and everyone looked happy and healthy and, well . . . glowing. Actually, literally glowing. At the head of the table was an elderly man with a long beard and an eye patch. Although his hair was white and his face wrinkled, he was also full of light and power, and he was roaring with laughter as he presided over the feast.

"A toast!" he shouted, and his voice was warm and rumbling (and, to Milo's relief, he was speaking in English, at least to his ears). "For Asgard!"

"For Asgard!" the gods repeated, and toasted each other with more laughter and clanking of goblets. "And to Odin!" they chorused, raising their glasses to the god with the eye patch.

"This seems like . . . a really good way to live," Alessia said, entranced. "Do you think someone can become a Norse god? Or is it like a have-to-be-born-into-it sort of deal?"

"The second option, I assume," Milo whispered. "But . . ."

"Halt!" Odin shouted, and the gods fell silent. "Who goes there?"

Both Milo and Alessia glanced over their shoulders to see who was approaching, before realizing it was in fact them that Odin was speaking to. They turned back slowly before Alessia straightened up and walked confidently into the courtyard.

"Great Odin," she said, and dipped into a deep and graceful curtsy, "we have journeyed to find you to ask for your assistance in a quest of great importance. We believe you are the only one who can help us."

Milo thought there would be more questioning of this, but Odin reacted as though it were normal for him to have people turning up asking for help with quests. Perhaps it was.

"Come closer, human child," he said, beckoning. "And your friend. Tell me your name and what you seek."

"My name is Alessia della Porta," she replied, walking toward the banqueting table. "And we need your aid to find something that will help us battle our enemy. He is a man of great power who seeks to take control of our world's imagination and use it to increase his own power and influence. He has already extended his life by many years more than is natural in his pursuit of this."

"He wants to live for eternity?" Odin spluttered, the thought of it clearly angering him. "It is not for mortals to live forever; that is not the way of things. He insults the gods in this."

It was apparent that this was a much more troubling thought to Odin than anything else Alessia had said, and so she wisely continued on that theme.

"He has no care for how things should be," she said. "He wishes to distort and steal and possess power and time that only the gods have been given before. With these, he will enslave the world's imagination, giving us no control over our own stories and ideas, and use it to increase his own power over the course of human progress."

"Hmph," Odin said, draining his goblet of wine. "I do not like the sound of this man; you have done well in coming to ask for our aid. What do you need to defeat him?"

"In order to separate him from the power he is stealing, we must use eitr," Alessia said, "the poison from the fangs of Jörmungandr."

"Jörmungandr?" Odin repeated. "I do not know that name."

"Ah," Alessia said, and Milo realized that wherever Merlin had sent them, it was before the gods learned of Loki's children.

"He is . . ." Alessia paused, clearly weighing up the risk of being the one to reveal the information. "He is one of Loki's children with the giantess Angrboda."

"WHAT?" Odin roared, getting to his feet and knocking several plates and bowls over. "Someone bring me Loki. Now! This makes some sense of the dream I had last night—a vision of three monstrous beings who had the potential to become great enemies of all of us here at Asgard. Where is that trickster?"

"I am here," said a slender, handsome man with long blond hair as he slid from the shadows. "You need not shout so loudly." He grimaced as if Odin's bluster were an embarrassment to him.

"Why are you skulking in the darkness?" Odin said, smoothing his robes and sitting back down. "Why not join the feast?"

"All this merriment gives me a headache," Loki said. "I have no appetite for mead and roasted meats today."

"But you do have other appetites," Odin said. "For mischief! Our young guest has told me things that echo strangely with the dreams sent to me of late."

At this, Loki's gaze slid like oil toward Alessia and Milo. There were mischief and malice in his eyes, but they shimmered together, as though he had not quite decided which he would let take precedence.

"And who might these children be?" he asked silkily.

"Never mind them," Odin said. "They are just mortals here to ask for aid. It is what they seek that troubles me, as it comes from one of your children."

"You know I have a son; this is no secret," Loki said. "Narfi is a good boy. I cannot imagine what these children need from him, but of course I will ask him to assist if he is needed, for he is an obedient child."

"Oh, come now," Odin spluttered. "Do not slither and slide as you insist on always doing. You know I speak of your other children, those you have made with the giantess Angrboda. The visions I have seen are of monsters."

"How cruel," Loki said, "to refer to my offspring as such. For their mother is the most beautiful of the giants, and she has borne me three strange—yes—but wonderful children. In fact, why not come to meet them yourself? You would be most welcome to visit Jotunheim and see that there is no need for you to concern yourself with them. And, along the way, perhaps I can hear more about what these two young travelers seek from them."

"We wish them no harm," Milo said, a nervous croak in his voice. "We had hoped to get some of the poison—"

But Loki cut him off. "No need to tell me now. There is plenty of time to speak along the way."

"Although I am vexed by your deception," Odin said with a yawn, seeming to tire of the subject already, "I see no reason why I should leave Asgard for this. I will send Thor, Sif, and Baldr to discover the truth of Loki's offspring, and you, humans, may go with them. Thor will protect you if Loki is tempted to mischief. That is my decision. There will be no debate. Now, let me feast!"

# 17

## Very Good at Quests

Odin tucked back into his food, apparently done with Milo and Alessia. But as he ripped a mouthful from a giant drumstick of some kind, a huge, broad, red-headed man at his right-hand side stood up and glared at Loki.

"Why must you always annoy me so, Loki?" he said, pulling his napkin from the front of his breastplate.

"Alas, it would seem I cannot help it, Thor," said Loki with a smirk. "And now we may journey together, which provides me with ample time to continue in that pattern. Have you considered relaxing a little?"

Thor only growled under his breath before turning to Milo and Alessia.

"Come," he said. "We have far to go, and we must endure the company of Loki. You can tell me more of your quest as we travel. Where is my brother Baldr and my wife, Sif?"

"Here." Two more unusually beautiful people approached from the other end of the table. They were both smiling and warm, and Milo found he was relieved they were coming too.

"I am sorry for my rude greeting before," Thor said to Milo and Alessia as they left the courtyard and walked back down the wide avenue. "I was enjoying my dinner very much, and Loki is always being bothersome and interrupting my feasting and storytelling. I am happy to assist my father, Odin, and you two, but I will not lie. I would prefer not to be traveling so far for such an unpleasant mission. For either Loki's children are indeed monstrous and will need to be captured, or they are innocents, and we will have to work out how to limit Loki's influence on them while also deciding whether to bring them back before Odin."

"Let us hope they are innocents," Baldr said. He was rosy-cheeked, golden-bearded, and gave off a distinct glow, even stronger than the others. "I am sorry I was not introduced to you properly," he said, bowing low to Milo and Alessia. "I am Baldr, god of the summer sun."

"That's a pretty cool thing to be," Milo said, and Baldr laughed.

"Cool, you say? Why, no, it is warm! You jest!" He gave a roar of laughter and clapped Milo on the back, propelling him forward a few steps.

"'Cool' is a word that means good," Milo explained awkwardly, as it was not a very funny joke if he had meant it literally.

"How fascinating," the goddess said. "I too must introduce myself to you properly before we journey together. I am Sif, goddess of the earth and wife of Thor."

"You have very beautiful hair," Alessia said, staring entranced at her unusually thick and lustrous golden hair. She wore a beautiful robe that trailed on the ground and yet didn't seem to get dirty, and she never tripped over it. A thin silver sword hung gracefully down her back in its scabbard.

"Thank you, child," Sif said graciously.

Milo felt quite absurd to be walking in such company. He felt extremely dull, short, and un-blond.

"What do you suppose we will find?" Thor wondered as they walked. "I hope I can use my hammer, whatever happens."

"There are few situations where you do not find something to do with it," Loki replied. "Whether it is required or not."

"I think we should prepare ourselves for the three children being fairly dangerous," Alessia said, as though she didn't already know. "But you know, we should also probably be nice to them because they're . . . Well, I'm not sure two of them quite count as people actually."

"It sounds as though you are well informed," Loki said. "Have you seen my children before?"

"No," Milo said truthfully.

"Will you tell us what you desire of them, at least?" Loki asked. "For I am sure we can come to some arrangement."

"Do not agree to any arrangements with Loki," said Baldr.

"It will always work in his favor. But I too am curious to know what you seek and why. I heard you tell my father that an enemy wished to be as a god?"

"Yes, sort of," Milo said. "In that he's made a potion that lets him live much longer than he should. He's trying to steal the world's imagination and has already managed to gain far too much control and can do things no one ought to be able to, but he still wants even more power."

"He wants to control everyone's thoughts," Alessia added quietly. "And direct them to make a world entirely designed for his own use and pleasure."

"That sounds grievous indeed," Sif said. "There is no mortal or god who is not enriched by their own imagination and that of others. We spend many happy hours sharing stories, and I know we inspire great tales among mortals."

"Now, I understand you coming to ask for our aid in your quest in a general sense," Thor said, "for we are most brave and beautiful. And I, in particular, am very good at quests. But you seem intent on a specific substance that will help you, and you already knew of Loki's children. I do not wish to question you too harshly, for you are but children yourselves, but how did you learn of these things?"

"We have a . . . guide," Alessia said. "A very wise wizard who is helping us. He was the one who suggested we come here. And we have . . . another guide, a woman who understands the magic of the world well, and she had a theory that we needed something so powerful that it could separate our enemy from his grasp on imagination."

"And they had both heard tell of your great deeds," Milo added.

"Of course." Thor nodded. "That makes a great deal of sense."

"And the wizard had a vision," Alessia said, trying to come up with the best way to explain. "Of Loki's children. A bit like Odin did maybe?"

"But Odin is guided by more wisdom than anyone else," Loki said. "He sacrificed his eye, in fact, to drink of the waters guarded by Mimir that spring from the world tree Yggdrasil itself. This wizard of yours must be very powerful indeed to receive the same visions as Odin."

"He is very powerful," Alessia said. "Perhaps the most knowledgeable wizard we have in our world. I am sure he's not as wise as Odin, though—of course."

"Or maybe he was also blessed with a vision from Mimir," Milo said, "because it was destiny that we should work together." He felt pretty proud of that one, and Alessia gave him a surreptitious thumbs-up.

"Yes, perhaps this is so," Thor said. "It makes little difference to me so long as I can use my hammer."

"You surprise me," said Loki sarcastically.

"You don't seem . . . worried about your children," Milo suggested tentatively.

"Do not presume to know what I am thinking," Loki said. "It will end ill for you. I have faith in Odin, as we all must, and we shall see what arises when we reach Angrboda's castle."

"Where is Angrboda's castle exactly?" Alessia asked as the group entered a forest. "In terms of distance or time. I don't mean to be rude, but we are in a little bit of a rush." Loki snorted at this.

"I actually have a terrible head for numbers," Thor said. "But it will not be too long—a few days, maybe a few weeks?"

"Right," Alessia said. "Do you make these sorts of journeys frequently then?"

"Oh yes," Thor said. "We are always off adventuring, taking great treasures, tricking beings who are less clever than we are."

"I see," Milo said, somewhat perturbed by Thor's good-natured but chaotic bluster. "I suppose time does operate a little differently if you live forever."

"Do not worry, children," Baldr said kindly. "We have plenty of provisions and can share stories and memories as we walk. Thor and I can carry you if you tire."

"That's very kind of you," Alessia said, and gestured for Milo to hang back a little so they could talk.

"I don't fancy spending a couple of weeks walking through the woods with Loki—should we read ourselves forward to where they actually find the children?"

"Okay, phew, I'm so glad you said that! Yes, good idea," Milo said in relief. "Let's hang back and check the book and get to the right bit."

Alessia flipped through the pages, then pointed out a line to Milo. It said that the gods "battled many dangers" on the way.

"Well, that decides it," Milo said. "Let's skip over that part."

"And they'll still remember us if we stay in the book, right?" asked Alessia.

"Yes," said Milo. "Or at least that's how it's always worked for me in the past. Have you found the right bit?"

"Okay, it just says that Odin sends some of the gods to find Loki's children and bring them to Asgard," Alessia said. "But, once they get back, Odin will take charge and cast the serpent into the sea, so I think we want to intercept it before then. Especially as the serpent seems to grow constantly, and we want to get it at the smallest possible point obviously. I also think it'll be easier to ask a smaller group of gods to help us— the other three seem friendly, I think? Or maybe we can do some kind of deal with Loki?"

"I'm not sure that's a good idea," Milo said immediately. "I know you're very persuasive, but he is famously deceptive. He's literally the trickster god."

"Okay, well, let's just see what happens," Alessia said far too easily. Milo knew her well enough by now to see through that.

"Alessia, promise me you won't make a deal with Loki without checking with me first?" he said.

"Fine, I promise. As long as you promise to seriously

consider it if need be. It might be that or going on a fishing boat and trying to catch a giant serpent."

"Okay, okay," Milo agreed. "Hopefully, it won't come to either of those things—let's get to the right bit."

"So just after they reach the giants' land then?" Alessia asked.

"Yep," Milo agreed.

"Let's hope the giants are friendly," Alessia said, and she read them forward.

When the world re-formed around them, they were out of the great forest, and the beautiful turrets of Asgard were nowhere to be seen. They stood in another courtyard, but that of a castle of dark stone, one that was definitely scaled bigger than human- or even god-size. Everything was square and solid and covered in frost. Milo and Alessia were grateful for their thick woolen clothes but were still shivering.

"You know that thing Merlin was saying about there being no limits to our imaginations?" Milo said, teeth chattering a little. "Do you think we can imagine ourselves to be wearing cloaks?"

"Worth a try," Alessia said, screwing her eyes shut and thinking hard, but no cloaks appeared. "It would have been useful if we could have imagined the eitr into our hands, but I suppose perhaps we're subject to the rules and the reality of wherever we are. We just have more control over where our imaginations take us. We're not in a dream after all: we're in a story that exists."

"Maybe we can ask Merlin when we get back," Milo said, rubbing his arms. "For now, can we please go inside?"

An enormous bang echoed around the courtyard and then a scream.

"I guess that's where we're going," Alessia said, and set off toward a huge set of wooden doors, one of which was open.

# 18

## Heroes and Villains

Climbing up the steps required a bit of a scramble as each one came up to their knees, but they made it and crept through the doorway toward the sound of the ruckus. There was another door open, this one hanging off its hinges, and beyond that was a kitchen. The cabinets were taller than Milo and Alessia, the whistling kettle on the stove the size of a beach ball, and the giantess the size of, well, a giantess. She was very beautiful, with intricately braided red hair, and stood half a meter taller than the gods, who were themselves considerably taller than the average human. Loki was nowhere to be seen, but Thor, Sif, and Baldr were facing off against the giantess and three very strange-looking creatures who cowered behind her.

From where they hid by the doorway, Milo and Alessia could see a teenage girl who looked scared and unintimidating—until she turned, and then they saw that while one half of her body was healthy and whole, the other was a mottled blue and black, and dead.

Her rib cage was visible on one side of her chest, and the bones in her arm and hand were visible. But despite this, she had the body language of a regular teenager, and Milo couldn't help but feel for her—she was obviously terrified. On either side of the girl were two animals—a huge, snarling wolf and a serpent that twisted itself around the girl to better see their enemies.

"I guess that's the one we need," Alessia whispered, and Milo felt rather nauseous at the thought.

"Do you think we can just ask it nicely?" he said. "Maybe it'll be happy to help. Maybe it's just frightened—to be honest, it doesn't seem especially fair that they're being taken away from their home."

At this point, the serpent let out a hiss, and a jet of black liquid spurted from its fangs. It didn't reach the gods, but the spot where it landed on the wooden table hissed and steamed, leaving a black burn mark.

"The good news is that that stuff is obviously powerful," Alessia said.

"Hopefully, Horatio actually knows what to do with it," Milo said. "I'm assuming we don't just chuck it at your father."

"I suppose chucking it at him is the backup plan," Alessia said. "One we might have to resort to if we can't get your uncle to wake up again. I don't understand why the cure only worked temporarily. It would've made some sense if it was all or nothing, but it's very strange that it woke him up and then just failed."

Alessia was distracted from her frustration by Baldr taking a step toward the giantess.

"Angrboda," he said gently, "we mean you no harm."

"I find that hard to believe, given the circumstances," she said in a low and husky voice. "Why are you here?"

"Odin has learned that you have married Loki and had these children with him, and it . . . displeases him," Baldr replied.

"I care not what Odin thinks of my relationships and my children," Angrboda said. "Do you do whatever Odin bids you, even if it means ripping apart a family who do not seek violence or indeed anything other than to be left alone?"

"Yes, actually, we do do whatever Odin bids," Thor said, as if this were a very clever rebuttal. "He is the Allfather, and we do not question his judgment. You would be wise to do the same."

"It amazes me that you are the beings given all the power," Angrboda said with a mirthless laugh.

"Do not mock Odin," Sif said. "He is wise beyond your comprehension."

"It is funny how one can be wise in some ways and in others, not at all," Angrboda said under her breath.

"Now, will you give us your children?" Baldr said, taking a step forward. "I will not lie to you: I do not know what Odin intends, but if it is as you say and they mean no harm, then I cannot see why he will not return them to you. But he has had a vision warning him of what may come to pass, and he does not trust Loki."

"In that we can agree," replied the giantess. "But no, I will not give you my children to be subjected to the whims of Odin."

"Then I regret that we must take them from you," Sif said, drawing her sword.

"Heroes and villains are less clear-cut than you'd think, aren't they?" Alessia whispered to Milo.

"Should we do something?" he asked. "Help them?"

"Help who?"

"I don't know," Milo said helplessly. "I suppose I meant the giantess and her children."

"I don't want to be on the wrong side of Thor's hammer," Alessia said. "And we already have them as allies. The story says they win, and it's our best chance of getting hold of the serpent's poison."

"It's horrible to watch, though," Milo said as the three gods started to advance on the giantess and her offspring.

"I know," Alessia said, "but it's what has to happen—it's what's written. Even if we made something different happen right now, as soon as we left the myth, it would just go back."

"I know," Milo said. "But that doesn't make it feel good to be part of it." And, even though Alessia was making a solid effort to remain impassive, Milo could see the discomfort on her face as they watched Thor raise his hammer and roar.

# 19

## Safe from Monsters

Despite Angrboda's best efforts, soon she was tied to a kitchen chair and had to watch helplessly as her children were taken captive. Hel, the half-dead girl, did not put up any resistance, and so they simply tied her hands, but the wolf, Fenrir, and Jörmungandr the serpent scratched and hissed until Thor subdued them, attaching a great chain of a leash to Fenrir and winding Jörmungandr around a great pole, securing him at either end, mouth bound closed, so he could be carried between two of the gods.

As Thor, Sif, and Baldr got the children ready to take back to Odin, Milo and Alessia heard a clucking noise behind them. They whirled round to see Loki leaning nonchalantly against the wall. He did not seem at all distressed by what was going on in the kitchen.

"Do you really not mind what happens to your wife and children?" Milo asked incredulously.

"Things will work themselves out," Loki said as if talking about missing a bus or losing his watch. "And, in my experience, what Odin wants, he gets, and to interfere with that only causes annoyance and inconvenience. I'll observe from a distance, and I will also naturally make sure Angrboda fares well. She protects the children more out of dislike of Odin than any particular affection—they are unusual creatures, let's be honest. She is wary of Hel in particular. You would be unwise to think Angrboda a kindhearted mother. And you two seek the poison of my son Jörmungandr, do you not?"

"Yes," Alessia said. "But we don't want to hurt him."

"I believe I can help you," Loki said. "Thor and the others will be focused on getting these three back to Odin, and wary of risking that purpose or harming themselves. I am your best chance of getting what you need."

"I'm sure that Thor will help us," Milo said firmly with a glance at Alessia to remind her of her promise. The three of them turned to see Thor helping himself to an apple cake in the kitchen, tripping over his hammer, and then giggling to himself, cake crumbs exploding from his mouth.

"Well, Sif then," Milo said. "Or Baldr." They looked back into the kitchen. Sif and Baldr were chatting merrily as they checked Hel's restraints, Baldr looking distastefully at her poor dead hand.

"They are too beautiful and too powerful to understand anything beyond their own beauty and power," Loki said. "If you are lucky and your goals align with theirs, you may get what you need, but there is no guarantee. They serve Odin, and they serve themselves. Thor is too easily distracted, and Sif and Baldr too focused on following orders. You need someone a little more . . . flexible on your side."

Milo and Alessia exchanged a glance. Milo was very nervous about putting their trust in Loki, who was notorious for his selfishness and for breaking his word. However, Milo knew there was a kernel of truth in what Loki said, and he could also see that Alessia was tempted—and she was very good at engineering situations to suit her goals. If there was anyone who could try and make a deal with the trickster god, it was Alessia della Porta.

"Of course, if I were to help you, I would need something in return," Loki said, sensing their softening. "A trinket, a tidbit, a promise, a favor."

"We don't trade in favors," Milo said immediately, remembering the way his uncle used sneaky promises and favors to suit his own, sometimes nefarious, aims. "And we don't have anything of value."

"It doesn't need to be riches," Loki said. "Not that I would turn down riches. But I am more interested in, well, interesting things. Come, I don't believe that two mortal travelers who have ended up in Asgard in search of Jörmungandr's poison are lacking in items of interest."

Milo was very aware that Alessia's backpack was full of

all sorts of interesting things, but they were not theirs to give away, and they might need them once they returned. He felt desperately in his pockets, but they were the woolen medieval clothes Bess had given him and so were empty of his usual bits and pieces except . . . What was that?

His fingers closed around the cold metal of the ring that he had pulled from the wall of Merlin's Cave back in Tintagel. Milo had forgotten that he had transferred it from his trousers to his tunic, intending to give it back to Merlin. It wasn't his any more than the items in Alessia's backpack were, but he felt more of a sense of ownership given that it was only because he was the Anonymous Reader that he'd been able to pull it from the rock in the first place. If it was so important, then surely Merlin would have asked for it back straightaway. Milo offered it to Loki.

"And what is that?"

"It's a ring belonging to the great wizard we spoke of," Milo said, aiming for some Alessia-style bluster to convince Loki it was worth helping them.

"Interesting," said Loki, nodding. "But what does it do?"

"Well," Milo said, trying to stall for time, "it is a ring of great note and importance and can only be found and used by the most . . . worthy of people." He cringed a little inside at calling himself that.

"Yes, yes, these things are always like that," Loki said impatiently. "But what does it do?"

Milo looked to Alessia in a panic. She shrugged. Even Alessia could not invent magical power for something.

"It does . . ."

And, in the hope that it might do something, Milo put the ring on. As far as he was concerned, nothing at all happened, but judging by Alessia's and Loki's reactions, something most definitely had.

"Milo?" Alessia called, spinning round, looking worried.

"I'm right here," he said, and she turned in amazement to where he was standing. Alessia stretched a hand out, and it thwacked Milo, who had not moved at all.

"You're invisible!" she said, entirely delighted.

"It is indeed charming," Loki said, also reaching out and poking Milo, rather less tentatively than Alessia. "But you do know I am a shapeshifter? I may not be able to render myself entirely invisible, but I can transform myself into a fish or a fly or something essentially invisible to the eyes of gods or mortals. Although true invisibility is not uninteresting . . . But I see you are willing to barter with something of actual value to you, and I appreciate that, young travelers. I am positive that we will be able to come to some agreement—you are sure there is nothing else that ring does? May I look at it?"

Milo took it off and, judging by the way Alessia started, appeared quite abruptly. He passed the ring to Loki and immediately regretted it. Catching the look that flitted across Alessia's face, she obviously regretted it too. Loki held the ring in the palm of his hand and studied it thoughtfully.

"There is clearly great power in this," he said. "It belonged to a wizard, you say?"

"Yes," Milo answered. "One of the most powerful."

Loki put the ring on his finger but stayed resolutely visible. He, however, clearly did not realize this and immediately made a very rude-looking gesture in the direction of the kitchen.

"We can see you," Alessia said dryly.

"Oh," said Loki, not looking at all embarrassed. "How curious. You try it." He gave the ring to Alessia, who slipped it on but also stayed defiantly visible.

"What makes you special?" Loki said, turning to Milo, a glint in his eyes that Milo did not like the look of at all.

"Nothing," he said immediately.

Loki laughed. "The evidence suggests otherwise. Are you sure you would not like to trade a favor?"

"Definitely not," Milo said firmly. "And we are more than happy to take our chances with Thor and Odin to get the poison."

"Do not be so hasty," Loki said. "You say this ring was created by your wizard?"

"Yes," Milo said.

"Well then," Loki said, "I will take it—I am content that it has power, and it is certainly interesting. I will take it to Sindri the dwarf and see what he makes of it; perhaps it can be melted down and made into something new, or perhaps we can work out how its powers might be used differently. Either way, it is interesting enough to please me, and I recognize it as a valuable item to you and therefore a sincere offering. It is enough to make a deal." And with that, he pocketed Merlin's ring and watched as Thor, Baldr, and Sif left the kitchen with their prisoners.

"We didn't agree to the deal yet!" Milo said.

"You did, by giving me the ring," Loki said with a smile. "Let me think on how best to retrieve the poison."

"I still think we need to ask the other gods first," Milo whispered to Alessia.

"Even though we've already lost the ring?" Alessia pointed out.

"I just don't trust him," Milo insisted.

"I understand," Alessia said. "Okay, there's no harm in trying the others while Loki's coming up with a plan."

"If he's even coming up with one," Milo muttered. "Maybe that's the last we'll see of him, or the ring."

Jörmungandr was bound too tightly to hiss or spit poison but was writhing on the pole he was attached to, held by Baldr and Sif at either end, while Fenrir, led by Thor, snarled from behind a muzzle. Hel was walking disconsolately next to them, hands still tied. None of the gods seemed particularly perturbed by the situation, but Baldr did notice that Milo was obviously uncomfortable.

"Fret not, child," he said kindly. "Your feeble hearts may struggle, but we will keep you safe from the monsters."

"Do you think they're okay, though?" Milo asked, realizing that Baldr had misunderstood his discomfort.

"Okay?" Baldr repeated.

"I'm worried that they're in a lot of pain," said Milo.

"Who?" Baldr asked in confusion.

"Hel and Jörmungandr and Fenrir."

"You know, the three tied up as prisoners?" Alessia said.

"Oh, do not worry about them," said Thor. "They are monsters, and we are gods—it is the way of things." He spun his hammer around his head with a flourish, a broad smile on his face.

"Do you know, one thing I've learned from bookwandering is that heroes of old are a little less heroic than they're made out to be," Alessia said as the procession moved back into the forest. "Very brave and strong, but not quite as . . . empathetic as you'd hope."

"It feels a bit unfair to criticize ancient gods and wizards for being a bit old-fashioned," Milo pointed out. "But some of these stories really are easier to enjoy from a distance, aren't they? I can see why people retell them. Should we go back and untie Angrboda?"

"I'm not sure adding an angry giantess into the mix is the best plan," Alessia said. "And remember that when we leave, it all goes back to how it has to be. We'd only be temporarily rescuing her, as well as making it harder for ourselves."

"Okay, but let's get the poison and go," Milo said. "I'm about done with this lot."

# 20

## A Little Unpredictable

Milo and Alessia quickly caught up with the strange procession and split up. Alessia took on Thor, as she was confident she could persuade him to do just about anything. Milo was tasked with speaking to Baldr, who seemed the most kindhearted, and both of them were keeping an eye on Loki.

"Tell me more about this enemy you wish to defeat," Baldr said to Milo, shifting the weight of the pole the serpent was attached to onto his other shoulder.

"He's a very powerful alchemist," Milo said. "And he seeks to control the world's imagination. He wants power over the most powerful people, over their stories and ideas and memories, so that he can be in total control. He thinks he knows best how to rule our world."

"And why does the poison from this vile serpent help you stop him?"

"I'm not completely sure yet," Milo admitted. "But I think the principle is that it's one of the only things powerful enough to separate him from the imagination that he's linked himself to. We have a friend who knows all about this stuff, but she's being held hostage by the Alchemist at the moment."

"Perhaps you could ask Odin if he would lend you Thor, and he could simply defeat this alchemist of yours with his hammer. If it is a bond that needs breaking, Thor and his hammer are an excellent solution, and Thor would happily aid you, I am sure."

"I wish that was possible," Milo said. "But it's not a physical bond, like a chain or a rope. It's all in the world of story and imagination—that's why it's so hard to work out how to break it. And anyway I'm not sure it's quite as easy as all that to get Thor out of Asgard, and given that he's . . ." Milo stopped, about to say that Thor was made of imagination so the Alchemist might have great power over him, but it wasn't polite to tell fictional characters they weren't real. "Given that he's very busy," Milo finished weakly.

"He is also a little unpredictable, I will admit," Baldr said with a sigh. "And easily distracted."

They both turned to look at Thor. Alessia was saying something to him, but mid-sentence he started tickling Fenrir under the chin (who seemed to be enjoying it, all things considered). Alessia saw them looking and gave a shrug of frustration. Milo returned his focus to Baldr.

"So could you help us get this poison, do you think?" Milo said. "It shouldn't be much bother—Jörmungandr seems pretty keen to spit it out, and Alessia will work out a way to catch it."

"But we would have to unbind his mouth."

"Well, yes," Milo agreed.

Baldr frowned. "I do not like the sound of that. I do not want to have that poison touch me."

"Don't worry, we'll figure out how to get it," said Milo. "I suppose we can even unbind his mouth if you don't want to do it. Odin did say you'd help us."

"Odin commanded us to bring the children of Loki back to Asgard," Baldr said. "He gave no specific instructions on whether or how to help you. I think it is best if we get back home and let Odin decide once he has seen these creatures. If he has said he will aid you, then you are fortunate indeed."

The gods were disconcertingly single-minded. Milo could see why people ended up making deals with Loki when he seemed to be the only one who saw things a little less black-and-white.

As if summoned, Loki strolled up to Milo.

"So we have our deal?"

"I suppose so," Milo said, ignoring his instincts. Perhaps Merlin would never ask for his ring back, and if he did, they would simply explain the situation and go from there. Merlin wanted the same thing as them, so he would understand.

"Very well!" Loki laughed. He didn't seem especially

worried by any of it, and not for the first time Milo thought that it was all just a game to him. Making a deal with someone like that was unsettling when it was anything but a game for him and Alessia.

"How are you going to do it then?" Milo asked.

"I have not quite decided yet," Loki said, watching the serpent thoughtfully.

"You said you were a shapeshifter?" Milo said, remembering Loki's earlier comments.

"An exceptionally talented one, yes."

"Well," Milo began, a plan coming to him as he spoke, "could you transform yourself into something very small maybe? Like a hamster?"

"A hamster?"

"Or a mouse," Milo said. "And then you could chew through the rope that's holding the serpent's head on the log. And then, as soon as he's free, you could change into a bird and fly away so you won't get eaten, and Alessia and I will work out a way to catch the poison before the other gods tie him up again?"

"You would need to be very fast," Loki said. "The others will not let his poison tarnish their beautiful clothes and faces— he will be bound anew almost as soon as he is freed. But I admit it is not an unclever idea."

"Thanks," Milo said, feeling proud of himself. He didn't trust Loki at all, but to be complimented by the trickster god for a smart plan still felt pretty good.

"Yes, that is what we will do," said Loki, nodding. "I suggest you go and ensure your friend knows how she intends to actually catch the poison—I cannot help with that. And I cannot predict, or control, how the other gods will react to the plan. Now, shall we proceed? I believe Jörmungandr grows bigger every time I look at him."

Milo made his way to Alessia's side. She was still trying and failing to maintain a conversation with Thor for more than a few moments at a time.

"I hope you're having more luck than I am," she said as Thor chased a butterfly into the trees with his hammer, pulling Fenrir on the leash behind him.

"Not with Baldr, who's dead set on not making Odin angry," Milo said. "But I agreed to Loki's deal."

"I knew you'd come round," Alessia said. "I definitely think he's the best bet because he'll do anything to annoy the others."

"What about the ring?" Milo asked. "What if it's important?"

"He's already got it," Alessia pointed out. "We can't worry about that anymore. So, what's the plan?"

Milo relayed his mouse idea.

"But we need to work out how to catch the poison," he said. "Loki isn't going to help with that bit. Is there anything in Rosa's kit that will help to contain incredibly toxic snake venom?"

"Of course," Alessia said.

"There is?" Milo asked in surprise.

"Rosa and your uncle have been thinking about how to

stop the Alchemist for longer than we have," Alessia said. "Considerably longer than you have, in particular. And you know that they've thought eitr might be the best bet for a while—it's why Rosa asked your uncle to get the poison cabinet after all."

"I suppose so," Milo said, once again impressed by how much Alessia paid attention to everything. Alessia shrugged the backpack off and crouched by it on the floor.

"We can't lose them," she said, "but I have what we need at the top." She pulled out a thick pair of gloves made of a material that was both leathery and sparkly, and a shimmering silver bottle. She tugged the gloves on.

"Kevlar gloves coated with distilled chimera skin," she said matter-of-factly. "Impervious to almost everything. And the bottle is made of silver, which can only be corroded by a few things, but it's been lined with the distilled bark of a tree that Rosa found in a fantasy book. It was called something like *The Four and a Half Beans of the Fishmonger's Daughter*, but the tree is resistant to acid—I don't know why a fishmonger's daughter would need that, but Rosa did say the book was pretty terrible. Anyway, the combo of the silver and the bark should do the trick."

"Should?" Milo repeated.

"I don't think anything else will work better," Alessia said. "Those are odds I'm happy to take, and I trust Rosa's research."

And Milo did too. In fact, he realized there was no one he trusted more, apart from maybe Alessia herself.

"You'd make a great assistant to Rosa," he said light-heartedly.

"Well, yes, that's the plan," Alessia responded casually. "Whatever happens, obviously I can't go back to Venice and live with, or without, my father. So I asked Rosa if I could stay with her and learn from her, and she said yes."

Milo wasn't sure why that made him feel so strange. It wasn't that he didn't want Alessia to live with Rosa—of course he did. She had nowhere else to go, and even if she did, Rosa was amazing and could do with some company. Alessia was also quite clearly very clever and loved learning everything Rosa could teach her. It made perfect sense. And yet the thought of it gave him a peculiar feeling all over, sort of queasy and itchy both at the same time.

Milo felt like he was being a bad friend not wanting that for Alessia, but he knew at least some of what he was feeling was rooted in the fact that he was avoiding thinking about what would happen to him. Horatio would probably be woken up again, and that was good, but it also meant that presumably they would go back to some version of the life Milo had had before: the two of them living on the Quip, doing some form of book smuggling. Hopefully, things would be a little friendlier and more open, given what they'd been through, and Milo thought he'd proven himself a bit by driving the Quip, but his uncle would not become a different person.

And that was the good option, the option where they

managed to defeat the Alchemist. If they didn't succeed in that, there would be far bigger things to worry about, and the Quip would probably be in the Alchemist's hands. The thought of that gave Milo the boost of energy he needed to stop worrying, at least for the moment, and focus on the task in hand.

Milo approached Jörmungandr, getting as close as he dared, as Alessia went to speak to Loki.

"Hi," Milo said awkwardly. "I'm not sure if you can talk when you're all tied up, but we don't want to hurt you. I know it really must seem like we're on the wrong side here, but we just sort of ended up in this situation because we wanted to talk to you. Can you . . . can you understand me?"

He looked at the serpent's yellow eyes, which were staring right into him. It wasn't clear if Jörmungandr could understand human speech, but he certainly knew Milo was communicating with him.

"Uh, right," Milo went on. "Well, we actually spoke to your dad, who is going to help us. So pretty soon you'll feel something on your head, and it'll be a mouse, but really it'll be your dad, and he's going to chew through the rope, and if you could sort of aim some poison at my friend Alessia, without hurting her, I'd really appreciate that. We need it to stop someone who wants to do really bad things where we're from. And although the whole concept of good and evil is feeling kind of topsy-turvy while we're here, I'm absolutely sure that he is bad, and someone who's definitely good told us your poison might help. So, yeah, that's the plan. Thank you if you can hear me and want to help, and I guess no worries if you can't. I hope that you . . . work it out with Odin."

"Are you talking to the serpent?" Sif said from her position at the front of the log Jörmungandr was tied to. She was laughing but not cruelly.

"Just checking in," Milo said, feeling embarrassed. "Can he understand us? He is the child of a god and a giantess, so surely he can. Although I don't quite understand how a god and a giantess made a snake. Or a wolf. Or . . . whatever is going on with Hel."

"We are not subject to the same rules that you are, human child," Sif said. "In life and death, or good and evil. And our children can be magnificent, or indeed strange, creatures. Loki himself is the child of a goddess and a giant, and he has unusual powers too."

"He can shapeshift," said Milo.

"Yes." Sif nodded. "To any living thing—an animal, a human, a woman. Be careful of him, for he is a trickster to his core and cannot act otherwise. It is a shame that we are not allowed to kill him."

"Why aren't you allowed?" Milo said, somewhat relieved to hear it.

"Odin and Loki are blood brothers," Sif explained. "So they have sworn not to kill each other, however much they both might wish to at times. Or however much we may wish to. But Odin clearly fears these offspring of Loki's and what they might signify, and his visions always contain at least a kernel of truth, even if veiled for the moment. We always heed them, and you would be wise to also."

"We honestly just want to get what we came for and be on our way," Milo said. "If you were happy to help us get some poison from Jörmungandr, then we wouldn't even need to talk to Loki. We could get out of your hair very quickly." At this, Sif touched her own luscious blonde hair protectively.

"What do you want with my hair?" she said.

"It's just a saying," said Milo. "It means that we'll get out of your way quickly. I promise we don't want anything to do with your hair."

"What's this about Sif's lovely hair?" Loki said, walking over with Alessia. Sif gave Loki a suspicious look and sped up, one hand staying on her hair as if to stop someone from stealing it right off her head.

"Right then," Loki said, a decidedly mischievous look on his face. "Shall we?"

Without waiting to see if they were ready, he vanished in the blink of an eye. Or rather he transformed, first into some flying thing too small for the eye to see and then into a tiny mouse that perched on the back of Jörmungandr's bound head. Milo saw the serpent tense as he felt the pressure on his neck, but he was bound so tightly that there was no way of knowing how he would react until he was free.

"I'd better get into position," Alessia said, and moved forward so she was level with Jörmungandr's head, walking next to Sif.

Milo watched mouse-Loki start nibbling through the rope that bound the great snake to the log. There was a wiggle of the mouse's tail that was Milo's cue to halt the group. He wished he'd thought about what he was going to do in advance, but with few options, he simply threw himself on the ground and yelled, "Ow!" The three gods stopped straightaway and turned to look at him.

"Are you well?" Baldr asked.

"Oh yes, sorry," Milo said, embarrassed. "I just tripped. Do you mind waiting a second while I just retie my shoe? Sorry to hold everyone up." He got to his knees and messed with his bootlace, hoping Loki had timed it right, and then, just as he was starting to worry that no one could spend so long tying a lace, there was a squeak and a snap and a hiss, and Jörmungandr's head was free.

# 21

## A Speedy Exit

There was a crash as Sif and Baldr dropped the pole carrying the serpent to the ground, not wanting to be in the line of Jörmungandr's poison. The snake writhed in the grass, unable to detach itself from the rest of its bindings. Thor jumped straight into action, passing Fenrir's leash to Baldr and approaching Jörmungandr's head, hammer held out in front of him.

But the serpent did not spit its poison, despite its obvious discomfort. Instead, it seemed to be searching for something from the forest floor. When it found what it was looking for, it lifted its neck as much as it could, and a jet of steaming black liquid spewed from its fangs in an arc, through the air and straight into the open bottle that Alessia was holding.

Everyone, including Thor, paused in surprise. Alessia speedily screwed the lid back on the bottle, and the five of them eyed each other, not quite sure what had just happened.

As usual in such moments, Loki was nowhere to be seen.

Milo stole a glance at Jörmungandr and would have sworn on the keys to the Quip that the great serpent winked at him. And then all hell broke loose.

Jörmungandr started writhing and twisting with great force, already almost twice the size he had been when they left the giantess's castle mere hours ago. He was shooting out poison as frequently as he could, and his efforts were sending Fenrir into a frenzy too, with Sif and Baldr struggling to keep hold of the huge wolf's leash. Hel was crying and distressed, standing to one side, apparently unsure who she most needed to keep out of the way of—her brothers or the gods. Eventually, all came to a halt when Thor gave Jörmungandr a firm bop on the head with his hammer, and the serpent stilled.

"He will be fine," Thor said. "It was only a tap to subdue him. It is for Odin to decide what to do with him."

"I think we should make a speedy exit," Alessia whispered in Milo's ear.

She had taken the chimera gloves off, and they, along with the eitr, were now stowed safely in Rosa's backpack. Alessia was holding the book she and Milo were inside of, and she grabbed his hand. Very quietly, she read the last line: "It was a sad story, but we tell it anyway," and, unnoticed by anyone, the two book-wanderers slipped away back to Arthurian times.

As the cozy wooden walls of Bess's inn reemerged, both Milo and Alessia started laughing in relief.

"Oh!" Milo said, stopping abruptly. "But what about Loki?"

"What about him? I don't think he'll remember us now that we're out of the book."

"But what about Merlin's ring?" Milo said.

"This ring?" Alessia said with a smile, holding it out.

"How on earth did you get that?" Milo said in delight.

"Turns out Loki's plan had one flaw: flies and mice do not have fingers big enough to wear golden rings. As soon as you told me the plan, I realized what would probably happen, so I was waiting, and the ring simply slipped off Loki when he first transformed, and all I had to do was pick it up off the grass and hope he didn't notice. I wondered if you'd thought of that on purpose."

"I wish," Milo said.

"You can say you did, to the others," said Alessia.

"I'll tell them it was a team effort," Milo replied. "Anyway, do flies even have fingers?"

"Actually, no," said Alessia. "That's a fairly horrifying thought, isn't it, a fly with fingers?" And they burst out into relieved laughter again.

Then, as they gathered themselves, it dawned on Milo that they were the only ones at the inn.

"My uncle isn't here," he said, all mirth immediately dissipating. Horatio was gone from the bench he had been lying on by the fire.

"Perhaps he woke up again!" Alessia said hopefully. "Or

maybe Bess had him moved upstairs to be more comfortable."

"And I guess Tilly and Oskar aren't back from trying to find the Muses," Milo added. "Hopefully, they're getting on okay."

"I'm sure they will be," Alessia replied. "They're pretty experienced at dealing with those kinds of situations. Shall we go and find Merlin? And Horatio?"

But neither of them were anywhere to be seen.

"That's got to be a good sign," Alessia said. "I knew my cure was right."

"In my experience, it's never a good sign to not know where my uncle is," said Milo. "He's usually doing something dangerous or illegal."

"I expect he's woken up and is with Merlin," Alessia said confidently. "Waiting for us."

"I hope so," Milo replied. "Let's find out."

The two of them headed out the main door of the inn. To their surprise, the door now led right into the courtyard in front of the great church, where the stone and anvil were, *The Book of Books* hiding within. The sun was nearly down, and the white stone gleamed in the twilight. There was no sign of Horatio, or even Merlin, but standing behind the stone was the Alchemist, and next to him was Archie Pages.

# 22

## Let's Keep Things Moving

ilo and Alessia froze. Although they had become quite adept at dealing with unexpected turns of events, finding the Alchemist and Archie here with Merlin and Horatio nowhere in sight tested even them. Especially as this was the first time that Alessia had come face-to-face with her father since escaping with Milo and Tilly, stealing his recipes in the process.

The Alchemist smiled coldly.

"Alessia," he said with a nod, as if he were meeting a colleague. "And Milo. We meet again, and how things have changed since we had dinner in Venice. Events could have progressed with significantly more ease if you and Matilda had simply agreed to work alongside instead of against me."

"You were going to . . . kill me," Milo said uncertainly. "That's not really working together."

"True, true," the Alchemist said, as if this were a minor

detail. "But that was when I thought you were merely the next in line to inherit your wonderful train. And more recently I have come to understand that you are a much more interesting proposition than that. Perhaps we should all be grateful my willful daughter helped you escape, otherwise I would have learned that fact rather too late to be of any use."

From this statement, Milo could only assume that the Alchemist had discovered that it was he, not Tilly, who was the Anonymous Reader. Perhaps someone at Pages & Co. had let it slip. But where were Rosa and the rest of Tilly's family? How had Archie gotten here?

And—most importantly—why was he not saying anything?

"Ah, you'll have noticed that our mutual friend Mr. Pages is spending some time in quiet reflection," the Alchemist answered, without needing the question spoken aloud.

"Mr. Pages, can you hear me?" Milo said.

Archie's mouth was moving, but they couldn't hear anything he was trying to say. He nodded, and then shrugged, which Milo took to mean, *Clearly, I am not okay—but having said that, I do not seem to be in any immediate danger.*

Milo took a cautious step closer and saw, with horror, that the stone of the courtyard seemed to have grown up out of the ground. Stony tendrils had emerged and wrapped themselves around Archie's legs, all the way up to his knees, meaning he couldn't move his legs at all.

"What is going on?" Alessia asked, and her voice sounded much smaller than usual.

"There's no need for either of you to understand much more than you already do," the Alchemist said. "Now, Milo, if you would be so kind as to retrieve *The Book of Books* for me."

"No," Milo said immediately and firmly.

"I thought it likely you would say that." The Alchemist sighed. "At least to begin with. As I have experienced with Matilda, you have decided that you must do the right thing, whatever that means to you. You believe that everything will be okay in the end, and you'll be able to protect your loved ones and somehow save whatever it is you think you're trying to save. Milo, through the regrettable incident with your grandmother, you've already seen that although I prefer to avoid unnecessary death, especially of powerful bookwanderers, I have no squeamishness about it. And you should bear in mind that it is not only Mr. Pages that I have here. Come forth."

And, from out of the shadows of the church doorway, Merlin and Horatio appeared, both walking as though they were being pulled toward the stone by a magnet. Horatio was awake, at least, but his eyes looked panicked, and he was clearly under the same spell as Archie because despite his mouth moving rapidly, they could hear nothing.

"Merlin, what's going on?" said Milo.

"I don't know how he got here," Merlin said, indicating the Alchemist, his face angry and worried. "He managed to open the gateway in the tree somehow. The way he has woven himself into the very roots of imagination is more powerful than I ever imagined. I should have listened to your warnings more carefully. I was able to resist him initially, but his powers exceed even mine."

"Now, I only allowed you to keep your voice so you could convince Milo of the severity of the situation," the Alchemist said. "There is no need for further explanation or exposition. Let's keep things moving."

"Milo, you must open the stone," Merlin said quietly, his voice shaking.

"What?" Alessia said in surprise.

"It is the only way," Merlin said. "If he destroys us all, then there is no hope. But, as I have told him, if his powers have reached this level already, I doubt there is anything in the Book that could even make much difference. Giving it to him will not worsen our situation. It is futile to resist him, and may only make things worse."

The Alchemist gave a dry laugh. "I understand your attempts to convince me of this, to make me disregard the Book's contents, but they fail to impress me. While my influence over the sphere of imagination has grown vast, there are secrets in that Book that remain locked even to me. I must own the power to create and destroy the magic inside people, and I must have the complete span of all knowledge. I must understand how this Book wields so much power in my world. But, Milo, don't let that change your course. You should listen to Merlin. Open the stone and give me the book."

"Where's Tilly?" Milo said to Merlin. "And Oskar?"

"They went . . . where they said they were going," Merlin said, keeping focused eye contact with Milo. "And they have not yet returned."

Milo wished he could just press pause and talk to Alessia and work out what to do, but there was no time. Was there any way to keep stalling the Alchemist until Tilly got back? Was there anything that Alessia could do with the eitr without Rosa's knowledge of how to use it? Alessia herself had made no move to take it from the backpack, and Milo decided to trust her instinct to keep it hidden.

"Okay," he said as he started walking slowly toward the stone, if only to give himself more time to think. "And what happens to us if I give you the Book?"

"I suppose that rather depends on what's inside it." The Alchemist smiled coldly. "But I see no reason to dispose of people who cannot stop me, or even those who might be persuaded to work with me, so let us proceed one step at a time, shall we? No need for you to worry about what happens next."

Milo looked back at Alessia, who shrugged helplessly. Her whole posture had changed in front of her father: shoulders bowed and hair falling over her face.

"Trust me, Milo," Merlin said.

Milo tried very hard to listen to his gut, but it was simply a swarm of distressed butterflies. He looked at Archie, then at Horatio, and realized there was no choice. He couldn't allow them to be hurt, so he would simply have to hope that Merlin knew what was best. Right now, the only way to protect them was to open the stone. So, as he had done earlier, he climbed up onto the marble and put his weight against the iron anvil. He felt it start to slide, and then it gained momentum and clanged down onto the ground.

"Why, thank you, Milo," the Alchemist said, coming over. "I think I need one further action from you: if you could just remove the Book and pass it to me. Merlin's protections are well created indeed, and I cannot even seem to raise my hand to try and take the Book from its hiding place."

Milo knelt on the stone and gently lifted the bound manuscript out. With a deep breath, he handed it to the Alchemist. Despite his affectation of calm, the Alchemist could not prevent a look of giddy delight from spreading over his face.

"I will remember your choice, Milo," he said. "I think you have been led astray by stronger voices than yours and that we may yet find a way to work together."

And that was when Milo knew he had made a mistake.

The Alchemist walked away from the stone and beckoned to Merlin.

"An excellent performance, sir," he said, laughing. "You almost had me worried you'd double-crossed me."

"It would not have served my purpose to do so," Merlin

said, straightening his back and leaving Horatio standing help-lessly by Archie. "These infants are in over their heads; I am relieved to find someone who can truly make use of the Book. Oh, and Alessia, I think it only fair to say that your cure worked perfectly. I just had to give Horatio here a little extra sleep before he told you too much. But well done!"

And with a wave of his staff, the stone tendrils rose up, and all four of them were trapped in the courtyard.

# 23

## A Few Chapters Ago . . .

After Milo and Alessia had vanished into Norse mythology, Tilly and Oskar turned to Merlin.

"Do you know exactly where you're sending us?" Tilly asked. "You said it had to be an English translation, which makes sense, but I'd like to know where we're going."

"Of course," Merlin said. "Although you should know that you will need to stray from the beaten path almost immediately. The Muses are rarely featured as characters in their own right. They do pop up, but they are the goddesses invoked by the great writers to tell their tales, not the heroes themselves. So I shall send you in at the start of things, where the Muses are always found—but you will have to make your own way, otherwise you might be sucked into the story that is unfolding. You need to stay at the beginning if you want to find Calliope."

"And can I imagine myself back, like I did in *The Railway Children*?" asked Tilly.

"You can go wherever your imagination allows you to," replied Merlin. "If you train it and can control it."

"So . . . controlling our imaginations is good?" Oskar asked.

"An interesting philosophical question, Oskar," Merlin said with a small smile. "Some might say no, that the power and magic of the imagination lie in its ability to be boundless, in its resistance to following any rules whatsoever. But, in my opinion, that depends on what you want to do with it. And if you want to travel wherever you wish, to take control of your own journey, then some level of training and discipline will be required. I am sure you understand. You both know the rules of bookwandering—that they were put there, at least in part, to keep people safe."

Tilly couldn't help but think of her mum, who had been punished for falling in love with a fictional character. Or the Source Editions that had been used by the Underwood twins to steal book magic.

"It is all about protecting imagination," Merlin concluded. "Now, are you ready?"

"What will you do while we're gone?" Tilly asked. "Is there any way to check to see if my family and Rosa are okay?"

"I am afraid I cannot see outside of imagination," Merlin replied. "I can only sense shifts in the imaginative web. But I will guard the gate until you two—and Milo and Alessia—have returned. But after that . . . well, here in my territory might be the best place to use whatever you can gather to defeat the Alchemist."

"Won't he be even more powerful here?" Oskar asked. "Like how you can do almost anything? And we need to speak to Rosa before we know what to do with the eitr."

"You raise some interesting points," Merlin said. "But this enemy cannot have amassed more power than me, I assure you. And, as I am unable to leave Story, you will have to choose whether you allow him here or whether you venture to Pages & Co., where yes, he will have less control over imagination. But so will you, and I will not be there to aid you. Although, of course, Rosa will."

"Well, we can worry about that when we get back," Oskar said. "It sounds like we haven't got a chance without the eitr and whatever Calliope knows anyway."

"Okay, yes," Tilly agreed, and then turned to Merlin. "We're ready. Send us to the Muses, please."

Merlin nodded and gave his staff a firm tap on the ground. As they were now used to, the cozy wooden beams of the Eyrie started to fold down around them, sucked into a spot beneath their feet. Once the walls of the inn had vanished, Tilly and Oskar found themselves high up among the clouds, in a palace of white stone. Wisps of cloud drifted past them, but despite how high up among the mountains they were, they could breathe normally, even deeply, for the air was fresh and clean and even tasted slightly sweet. They were standing on a bridge that connected two tall turrets. A sparkling waterfall spilled down the rock face on one side of the bridge. Lush flowering trees covered the rocks and buildings, and birdsong mingled with the sound of splashing water.

"I guess this is Mount Olympus," Oskar said. "Home of the gods."

"How do we find the Muses?" Tilly asked, looking around her. "I can't see anyone at all." At that point, the sound of laughter echoed from somewhere nearby, and Tilly saw the silhouette of a broad-shouldered man on a balcony of one of the towers.

"Something's happening," she said. "How do we make sure we stay at the beginning?"

"We use our imaginations," Oskar said, taking hold of her hand. "We need to stay where Merlin sent us. Focus on the moment we arrived!"

Tilly held on to Oskar's hand tightly and concentrated on staying at the beginning, trying to resist the story moving forward, and a strange thing started to happen. There was a blurry look to the air, a shimmer like heat haze, and then the waterfall started to flow backward.

The *water rushed* from the pool upward into the rocks, as if on rewind, and the figure on the balcony disappeared. It was like when they'd been at the very end of *Alice in Wonderland*, and everything had started to rewind around them when they reached the end of the book. After a very strange few seconds, everything righted itself, and the waterfall ran the correct way.

"I did not like that," Oskar said, shivering a little bit. "But it worked!"

"It's almost frightening how much more control we have in stories than we think," Tilly said. "It doesn't really quite fit with everything we've been told about how bookwandering works, you know."

"But people have said that sort of thing to us before, haven't they?" Oskar pointed out. "That there are rules and limits in places that don't need to be there. People we trusted and people we didn't. It's why we freed all the Source Editions, isn't it? Because they didn't need to be kept locked up like that."

"I hope Calliope has some answers," Tilly said. "And about more than just how to stop the Alchemist."

"We've got to find her first," Oskar said. "Can we imagine ourselves to her? If we both try together maybe?"

"I don't really know how to imagine myself somewhere I don't know anything about," Tilly pointed out. "I've only managed to do it to get to places I can picture—sort of like when Milo drives the Quip. You have to be able to imagine where you're going in some sort of way. I don't know how to imagine the Muses."

"Not going to lie, I'm thinking of the Muses in the Disney *Hercules* film," Oskar said. "I hope they're like that—imagine if we were in a musical. That would be awesome."

"I hope so too, but I'm worried they'll be a little less friendly. I wonder if . . . okay, don't laugh, but you know how

Merlin said the writers, like, invoke the Muses when they start to tell a story? Should we do that?"

"I don't even know what 'invoke' means," said Oskar, laughing.

"I think it means to sort of ask them for inspiration," Tilly said. "Will you laugh if I try it?"

Oskar grinned. "I can't promise that I won't. It depends on what you say!"

"You either have to do it with me or turn round and put your hands over your ears," Tilly said. Oskar went to do the latter, and Tilly felt embarrassed, but then he turned and smiled.

"I'm joking!" he said. "Of course I'll do it with you! I just don't know what to say . . ."

"I'll start, and you sort of join in on that vibe?" Tilly said. "I figure we're basically just asking the Muses, and Calliope in particular, to show up and help us tell our story. I think that's what people like Homer did. Okay, here goes. Uh. Calliope? If you can hear me, then please could you come and help us? We're here to ask for your . . . your knowledge and your inspiration so we know how . . ." She tailed off and looked at Oskar.

"So we know how to finish our story," he continued, looking uncertainly at Tilly, who nodded enthusiastically. "Right," he went on. "Yes, please come down from whichever turret you live in and help us, because without your wisdom and . . . and . . ."

"Without your wisdom and kindness"—Tilly took over—"we have no hope of guiding our story to its ending. So, yes, if you wouldn't mind being invoked, if that's how you say it, we'd really appreciate it."

"Cheers," Oskar finished off. They looked at each other and started giggling.

"It was worth a shot!" said Tilly.

"Absolutely," Oskar said. "But if Calliope responds to that, then I honestly might question her judgment."

"And why would you question the judgment of a goddess responding to a sincere plea for inspiration?" a voice like silk and honey said from behind them.

# 24

## Chief of the Muses

Tilly and Oskar whirled round to see a woman standing at the end of the bridge. She was tall and beautiful with broad shoulders and olive skin. Her hair was dark brown and fell in luxurious waves over her shoulders. A delicately woven circlet of golden leaves adorned her hair, and a one-shouldered dress of cream linen was gathered at the waist with more golden leaves. She did not smile at them, but her stance was not frightening either, more curious.

"Who are you?" she asked, taking a step toward them.

"My name is Tilly, and this is my friend Oskar," Tilly replied politely. "We were only laughing because we thought we'd gotten it all wrong."

Calliope tilted her head to one side as if confused.

"But you asked for my help?" she said. "I am the chief of the Muses, and you invoked my assistance, so I have come. I must admit, usually the writers and poets who call on my name do not request a personal visit, but the . . . style of your request was so unusual that I was curious to see who had summoned me in such a fashion."

"We didn't mean to be disrespectful," Oskar said. "That is, if you felt it was disrespectful? Did . . . did you think it was disrespectful?" Calliope watched them with her large dark brown eyes, and then finally smiled.

"Be at peace, child," she said. "Come and meet my sisters and tell me more of why you have asked for my assistance."

She held out her hands, and Tilly and Oskar walked across the bridge and took one each. The shining columns of the palace melted away, and they found themselves in a grand hall. Although "hall" was not quite the right word, Tilly thought to herself, for there was no ceiling. Bright white stone columns surrounded a circle of flagstones, but there was nothing resting on the columns but golden baskets and vases full of luscious green vines that tumbled down the stone, and huge, bright flowers of pink and yellow. The sky above was a beautiful wash of pink and blue, as if permanently held just before the sun began to set. And in a semicircle, each sitting on a throne, were eight women.

Although Calliope had referred to the other Muses as her sisters, none of them were alike. They had different skin and hair colors, but all looked about the same age. Each throne was different too. The one to the right of Calliope was made of golden manuscripts, with one unfurled to form a seat. Another seemed to be constructed from feathers, one was the shape of a lyre, and one was made of leaves, all rendered in gold.

"Meet my sisters," Calliope said as she took her seat on the central throne. She gestured from one end of the semicircle to the other and introduced them in turn. "Thalia, Muse of comedy; Melpomene, Muse of tragedy; Terpsichore, Muse of dance; Clio, Muse of history; Euterpe, Muse of music; Erato,

Muse of love poetry; Urania, Muse of astronomy; and finally Polymnia, Muse of hymns."

As each of them was introduced, they nodded or smiled or frowned at the two bookwanderers before them.

"Now, you have called on us, on me specifically," said Calliope. "What is your tale? Is it one you are about to begin?"

"It's one we're sort of in the middle of," Tilly said, feeling extremely human and scraggly in the middle of a group of such ethereally beautifully people. "We are mortals."

"That much is obvious," Melpomene said under her breath, making Thalia giggle.

"Right, yes, obviously," Tilly said, embarrassed. "Anyway, there's a man who is trying to steal the world's imagination. He has linked himself to it somehow and wants to control it entirely and enslave us all to his will. Our world will become his, all our ideas a battery for his power. And we were told that you could help us."

"Help you in what goal?" Calliope asked.

"Stopping him," Oskar said. "I would've thought you'd be pretty invested in making sure imagination stays out of the hands of evil people."

"It would not affect us too deeply," Urania said slowly.

"But, sister, it already is, you know it's true," Calliope said.

"What?" Tilly asked in surprise. "You already know?"

"I know in my bones that something is wrong," Calliope said. "In a deep and terrible way. I can feel that someone is tampering with the very roots of imagination, the roots that we planted and watered. Someone has stolen things that are not theirs to take."

"Yes," Tilly said in excitement. "You do know! It's a man who calls himself the Alchemist."

"No," Calliope said. "It started before that."

"He's been alive for a very long time," explained Tilly. "He's been using imagination to extend his life."

"I can feel the wrong that this new enemy is causing, but he did not start the decay."

"Then who did?" Oskar asked.

Calliope was silent for a moment, studying them deeply.

"If you do not already know, then how can you hope to defeat them?" she asked after a long pause.

"Well, I think we can defeat the Alchemist," Tilly said uncertainly. "Which would be a good start, right? And you say that you can feel what he's doing too, so whatever else is going on, this needs fixing. So if you tell us more about the other thing, maybe we can help with that too?"

"It would require someone with the deepest understanding of story and imagination," Calliope said. "Is that you?"

"No," replied Tilly. "But me and my three friends together? Then I think we stand a pretty good chance, actually."

# 25

# The Goddess of Memory

If you and your friends wish to defeat this ancient enemy," Calliope said carefully, "then there are three . . . I will not call them tests, but there are three places that I wish you to journey to so I know that you truly understand the nature of what we speak. You have no hope of battling against what you do not understand. Although please take courage from the fact that I have great faith in you, children. That you will be able to perceive what you need to. And I have faith in the sincerity of your purpose, something my sisters and I admire and respect. Will you take these journeys I put before you?"

Tilly looked at Oskar. She wasn't sure what other choice they had. He nodded his agreement.

"We will," they said together.

"Very well," Calliope said with a warmer smile. "First of all, I would like you to come and meet our mother. This is your first journey."

"That is significantly less scary than I thought," Oskar whispered to Tilly as Calliope looked around at her sisters.

"Depends who her mother is," Tilly pointed out. "You can't trust anything in these myths. It could be a monster."

"She is no monster," Calliope said gently, and both Tilly and Oskar blushed that she had overheard them. "Her name is Mnemosyne, and she is the goddess of memory. Come."

The council of the Muses melted away, and a great library emerged. It reminded Tilly of the Library of Alexandria—airy and bright and full of shelves stacked with rolled-up manuscripts. At a desk sat a woman with shining white hair, writing with a sharpened reed dipped in ink. She was eating from a plate of grapes as she worked, and when Calliope arrived, she looked up and smiled.

"Calliope, you have brought me guests," she said in a low, melodic voice. "What a pleasant surprise. Although a surprise, indeed, that you have brought two mortal children to Mount Olympus."

"They found their own way here," Calliope said with a raised eyebrow.

"Even more surprising," Mnemosyne replied, putting down her pen and standing up. She was as tall and elegant as Calliope and her sisters. "How did you make your way to the palace of the gods?"

"We didn't really realize we were coming here," Tilly tried to explain. "We were told by a . . . well, he's not quite a friend, more a guide. Or a mentor? He's probably not quite . . . patient enough to be a mentor. I do think he's essentially on our side, though, and—"

"And what did this not-quite-friend tell you?" Mnemosyne prompted gently.

"Sorry, yes," Tilly said, feeling nervous and inarticulate. "He said that we had to come and find Calliope, that she was the person who could tell us how to stop the Alchemist."

"That is what he said precisely?" asked Mnemosyne.

"No, I suppose not precisely," Tilly said, looking at Oskar for reassurance.

"He said we needed to go back to the very beginning," said Oskar.

"Yes," Tilly said, trying to bring Horatio's exact words to mind. "And actually, yes, he said we had to go back to long before the Alchemist started doing what he was doing. But then he fainted, or was poisoned, or maybe stayed poisoned, we're not quite sure, but he couldn't tell us any more."

"An interesting tale," Mnemosyne said, more to Calliope than to Tilly and Oskar. "Do you think we may finally be able to achieve what we have spent many centuries striving for?"

"I am hopeful, Mother," Calliope replied. "But while these two are, I believe, pure in heart and intent, they have not been furnished with the information they need. I have brought them to you, and I will send them to speak with the others, and then . . . Well, let us see what happens."

While it is usually considered quite rude to talk about someone who's standing right there, Tilly found it hard to resent the two Muses. They knew what she needed to know, and she realized she was willing to do whatever was asked of her to find it out and help. Despite his previous actions, she believed that Horatio had told them the truth about this being the missing clue.

"My mother is the goddess of memory," Calliope said. "She cares for what has been, not just the acts, but the way they are preserved and treasured. Have you thought before about why we remember some stories and not others? You said you had to come back to the very beginning—but we are not even at the very beginning. There are stories even older than us, like that of Gilgamesh, and many others that are lost. We are the most ancient guardians that still remain, but there are others from different times and places. As long as there have been humans, there have been stories, even if they are not always remembered. There is never just one story, or one history."

"So . . . you know you're a story?" Tilly asked.

"I think that if you have come as far as this, child," Mnemosyne said, "then you are beyond such questions."

"I know," Tilly said quietly. "But . . . I'm half made of story, and I've never quite known what that means."

"Ah," Calliope said kindly. "Then it is no wonder you found your way to Mount Olympus. You have a bit of us in you."

"A bit of goddess?" Tilly said in wonder.

"Of a kind," said Calliope, smiling. "Certainly a portion of what we are made of."

"Which is hope and starlight and whispers," Mnemosyne added. "And imagination, of course."

"Pretty cool," Oskar murmured.

"The next parts of your journey will help you understand this further," Calliope said. "It is to aid you in thinking about who you are, and what stories are, and what they mean. And this is why we have started here with my mother, in her library. With memory and the past, and the stories that have come before us. The next place you must travel to, you will go by yourselves. It is more dangerous, but you will know what to do, and when you find the end, you will be taken to the third place I wish you to see."

"And then you'll help us?" Tilly asked.

"And then you will be able to help yourselves." Calliope smiled. She kissed her mother on both cheeks, and then kissed Tilly and Oskar on the tops of their heads. With that, the library of Mnemosyne started to shimmer and was replaced by a far more unpleasant setting.

# 26

## Follow the Thread

They stood in a cold, dank stone room without windows. Water dripped lazily down its walls, and it had only one door, a great wooden one that was locked. But they were not alone. They were among a group of scared and shivering teenagers—seven boys and seven girls. Despite their current situation, they all looked healthy and well fed, as if this change in circumstance were very new. One man, who was particularly hale and golden, was speaking confidently at the center of the group.

"Do not lose courage, fellow Athenians," he said. "I will enter the labyrinth of the Minotaur first and save us all. You will all be safe, and I will rid our nation of this vile tax of human life that King Minos exacts."

"Ah," Tilly said, feeling rather scared, "'Theseus and the Minotaur.'"

"What are we supposed to do?" Oskar asked. "I don't want to meet the Minotaur."

"Me neither, obviously," said Tilly. "But I can't imagine that Calliope wanted us to just stand in this room with the other prisoners and wait. I think we're supposed to go with Theseus into the labyrinth."

"We'll be fine, though, right?" Oskar said, a slight shake in his voice. "Theseus was fine."

"Yes," Tilly replied, trying to sound like she believed it. "I don't think Calliope would have sent us to our deaths—we have to trust her. We'll just stick close to Theseus."

At that moment, the great wooden door swung open, and several soldiers appeared.

"With me!" one shouted. "King Minos wishes to see you before you enter the labyrinth."

Amid the cries of distress from the group, Theseus remained calm.

"Fear not, friends," he said. "Follow me." The soldier gave him a dismissive look and roughly pushed him through the doorway, making sure the rest followed.

"Halt!" another soldier said as Tilly and Oskar filed past him. "You are too young to have been sent." He did a quick head count. "And surplus to the numbers required." He lowered his voice. "I don't know who you are or how you arrived in this godsforsaken place, but you'd best get out as quickly as you can. It is not an honorable fate that awaits these youths. Follow me and I will try to lead you somewhere you can make your escape. You should find a ship to buy passage on, or stow away on, and sail back to your families as quickly as you can."

"Thank you," Tilly said, "but we have to follow Theseus."

The soldier looked uncomfortable, and while she was appreciative, Tilly wished he felt as uncomfortable about the young Athenians who were about to be sacrificed.

"King Minos will not allow it," he said. "He won't like the numbers to be different. And if he were to see you, he might wish to keep you as slaves—your clothes show you are not Cretans."

"Please can we just sort of tag along for a bit?" Oskar said, seeing the group of victims being led farther away. "And I promise we'll sneak away at the right moment."

The soldier clearly didn't want to put them in any danger, but neither did he want to risk his own job or life.

"It's of no mind to me what you do," he said eventually with a sigh, straightening his back. "But I warn you: none return from the labyrinth. And many who were stronger and older than you have entered. Now we approach King Minos, but I do not think things will go well for you if you are noticed."

He followed the group of Athenians up a long set of stone steps and through an increasingly luxurious succession of hallways. Theseus was leading, and the other young people were too frightened to notice Tilly and Oskar among them. The other soldiers either didn't notice or didn't care.

Eventually, they arrived at a grand throne room lined with staring nobility who were draped in fabrics dyed in rich colors, and adorned with gold jewelry. The room itself was paved in white stone, and an elaborate mosaic in different shades of red tile covered the walls, depicting a battle scene full of gods and goddesses.

At the far end of the room, on an imposing throne of gold, sat a man of about fifty. He had dark hair peppered with gray and wore a thick white robe with a deep red sash clasped with gold at his shoulders. A sword hung from his waist, and a circlet of gold leaves was atop his head.

Behind his throne, Tilly caught a glimpse of a dark-haired head poking round to look at the prisoners. A young woman, around the same age as the victims, appeared distressed as she gazed at them assembling. The king noticed her and said something sharply, and the head retreated back into the shadows of the draperies behind the throne.

As the group of sacrifices walked into the room, a hush fell over the watching people, and the soldiers shepherded the Athenians forward until they stood before the king.

"Kneel," he commanded.

"No, sir," Theseus said without even the suggestion of a waver in his voice. "We will not. I am Prince Theseus of Athens, and these are nobles of Athens. Though we stand before you as prisoners, we will not kneel to you and your cruelty. I intend to end this evil arrangement that you have forced upon us."

King Minos looked Theseus up and down and started to laugh.

"Impudent young thing," he said. "You may carry those naive beliefs with you into the labyrinth, where my Minotaur will disabuse you of them quickly."

"Your Minotaur indeed," Theseus said. "For I hear it is your great shame, a monstrous child born to you, a symbol of your cruelty sent by the gods themselves."

That wiped the smirk from Minos's face, and he stood, his face like stone.

"Enough!" he shouted. "I will forgive your wailings and rumors in light of what awaits you, but I find myself bored of this charade. Take them away, and I shall remind King Aegeus to send less troublesome tributes next time."

Theseus looked as though he wanted to argue more, but the king left the dais to speak to a nobleman nearby, and the soldiers quickly started moving the group back out of the throne room. As they left, Tilly noticed that the young woman behind the throne had darted out and was following them, drawing as little attention to herself as Tilly and Oskar were trying to.

On exiting the throne room, instead of following the corridors back toward the cell they had arrived in, the group was led along a different route that ended in many, many stairs disappearing down into the dark. A frightened silence surrounded them now, and even Theseus was quiet. Only the sound of sandals on stone and the clanking of the soldiers' armor could be heard.

"Are we sure this is a good plan?" Oskar whispered to Tilly, looking very scared. "Surely this isn't what Calliope wanted us to do?"

"I don't know," Tilly said nervously. "But we can imagine ourselves out if things get too . . . hairy. We can go back to where we first arrived, or even back to Merlin if we have to. Let's keep going for now . . . I want to see what Calliope sent us for."

At that point, a small, cold hand grabbed Tilly's, and she turned to see the girl from the throne room next to her, head bowed to avoid notice. She was easy to miss, as the clothes of the Athenians were nearly as fine as hers.

"Here," she whispered, and pushed a ball of red thread into Tilly's hand. "Use this to keep track of where you are going, and you will be able to find your way back." She tried to melt away again, but Tilly caught hold of her wrist.

"Are you . . . Ariadne?" she asked.

"I am," the girl said, looking scared. "And I should not be here. But I had to try and stop my father's cruelty when I saw the tributes." She sighed. "The beautiful prince of Athens himself sent to such a terrible fate."

"Do you want to give him the thread, maybe?" Oskar suggested.

"I think you will be able to guide the others," Ariadne said. "Just follow the thread and keep going. The labyrinth may seem endless—it was designed by Daedalus after all—but it has a way out and a purpose, I swear."

And with that, she shook herself free of Tilly's grasp and

disappeared into the shadows, just as the group reached a huge doorway closed with a portcullis.

"I will go in alone," Theseus announced bravely, but Tilly could see the sight of the dark corridor stretching away beyond was frightening even to him.

"No, you won't," the soldier said with a grim laugh. "You're all to go in together. What you do in there is up to you." He took hold of a great chain to the side of the door and heaved on it until the portcullis began to creak upward, revealing sharp spikes that fitted into slits in the floor. When it was above their heads, he gave a jerk of his chin.

"In," he said. "And may the gods have mercy on you."

"And you, for your part in this," Theseus said, holding the soldier's eye. "Onward, friends," Theseus continued, and led the group into the gaping mouth of the labyrinth.

Tilly and Oskar kept close to the center of the group, Tilly holding on tightly to the ball of thread. Once they were all through, the soldier let go of the chain with a grunt, and the portcullis slammed back down into the stones, leaving them alone in the darkness.

# 27

## Dramatically Weird

The footsteps of the soldiers echoed into nothing, leaving them in silence apart from the drips of water down the walls.

"Gather round," said Theseus, and it was then that he finally noticed Tilly and Oskar. "You are not Athenians," he said. "How did you end up with those of us forgotten by the gods—has King Minos's cruelty extended to sending even younger children of his enemies here?"

"Yes?" Tilly said, feeling as though that was probably the easiest explanation.

"He is evil indeed," one of the other Athenians muttered. "For we are all doomed."

"No," Theseus said. "I wish for you all to stay gathered here so that you do not lose yourselves within the labyrinth. I will do battle with the fearsome Minotaur myself, and if the gods are on my side, I will return to you."

"But, even if you survive, how will you find us again?" one of the Athenian girls asked.

"Oh"—Theseus paused—"I actually had not thought of that."

"We can help!" Tilly said, and held out the ball of red thread. "The princess Ariadne gave this to me. She doesn't agree with her father, and I think would be quite keen to get out of Crete actually, if you had space for her on the way back. But look, tie this to the portcullis, and let it trail behind you as you go, then you'll be able to find your way back."

"A very clever idea," Theseus said, taking the thread and knotting one end firmly to the portcullis bars. "You said her name was Ariadne? Was she beautiful?"

"Excuse me?" Tilly said in surprise.

"Was the princess beautiful? You said she wanted to escape this island, and I thought perhaps if she was beautiful, I could marry her."

"There is . . . so much wrong with that," Oskar said. "And when you add the timing in . . . Wow. There are perhaps more important things to be thinking about?"

"More important than beauty and love?" Theseus said, sounding genuinely confused.

"Yes?!" Tilly said. "Right now, more important than love. And most of the time when it comes to beauty."

"Right now, the priority is escaping the labyrinth and rescuing these people," Oskar said, and gave Theseus a gentle push into the labyrinth. After he had ventured a little farther in, Tilly and Oskar started to follow the red line he left in his wake.

"These mythical people are always so dramatically weird," Oskar said. "I'm not sure what Calliope wants us to learn from someone like him."

"It might not be him in particular," Tilly said. "Maybe we have to find something in here. Something that's not the Minotaur? It reminds me of that labyrinth we nearly had to go through to get to the Archive—do you remember? But we'd lost our red thread. Thank goodness we ended up catching a lift on the Quip—everything might have turned out so differently if we'd never met Milo. Who knows what the Alchemist might have managed to do if we hadn't all teamed up? I hope Milo and Alessia are getting on okay with the Norse gods."

"If anyone can convince a mythical serpent to give them some really poisonous venom, I imagine it would be Alessia," Oskar pointed out.

The red thread led them through a tortuously complicated maze of stone. They kept enough of a distance that Theseus could double back from any dead ends without bumping into them, for there were many false turns and blocked-off corridors. There were also passageways that seemed to get narrower and then wider as they walked, making Tilly feel dizzy like at a carnival hall of mirrors. Without the thread, Theseus would have had no chance of finding his way back out, even if he succeeded in besting the Minotaur. Of course, the myth said that he would always win and that Ariadne would always help him, and Tilly and Oskar had to trust in that. At first, Tilly feared they would be following the thread for a very long time, but then the sound of a terrifying bellowing and the scraping of hooves and horns could be heard.

And it was getting closer and closer.

"Uh, what happens if we meet the Minotaur before Theseus?" Oskar whispered at the sound of a roar that was very near.

"I guess we imagine really hard that we're somewhere else," Tilly answered, swallowing nervously. The thread led them into a square opening, the walls marked with deep scratches and blood.

"Where are you, foul beast?" Theseus's voice echoed, and he emerged back into the square, retracing his steps into this opening, where so many signs of the Minotaur were. "Come and face me!" And at that, there was another great roar and a clatter of hooves on stone, and in burst the Minotaur itself.

Tilly and Oskar flung themselves back round the corner and hid as the beast appeared, pawing at the floor in rage. Tilly's heart was beating incredibly fast as she and Oskar pushed themselves hard against the wall to avoid attention. But the Minotaur and Theseus were focused solely on each other. Tilly and Oskar could only listen, hands over their mouths, to the sounds of the battle. Scrapes and roars and grunts and horrible noises that Tilly could not quite understand.

The fight raged for a long time, until finally there came a slash and a heavy thump and an exhausted cry of success from Theseus. Tilly poked her head round the stone wall to see the Athenian prince, covered in blood, leaning against the Minotaur, who was vanquished and lying lifeless on the ground. Theseus was breathing heavily and did not look in the best way himself; the Minotaur's horns had clearly found purchase during their fight. When he caught sight of Tilly and Oskar, he didn't have the energy to protest very much.

"How did you find me here in this cursed place?" he said raggedly.

"We followed the thread," Oskar said.

"Of course," Theseus replied. "And now we must follow it back. Will you aid me?"

Tilly and Oskar helped him up as best they could. Managing to get one of Theseus's arms draped over each of their shoulders, the awkward trio set off, following the red thread on the stone floor. It was hard going: the maze seemed endless, even longer than when they had come in. Twists and turns splintered off from every corner; there would have been no hope at all if it weren't for that slender glimmer of scarlet on the ground.

Theseus occasionally dipped out of consciousness, but when he was able, he supported himself as best he could. Tilly knew that they could leave at any point, imagine themselves somewhere easier, but regardless of the journey set for them by Calliope, it did not feel right to abandon Theseus, even if his story dictated that he would find his way back without them. They simply had to keep going.

Just when Tilly thought they could not go any farther, the sound of the scared group of Athenians could be heard, and they knew they were finally drawing close.

"Help!" Oskar shouted as they stumbled onward with Theseus barely conscious between them. There was a pause in the chattering as if the waiting people could not believe what they were hearing.

"Help!" Tilly repeated desperately. "It's Theseus and he's wounded! Follow the thread!"

At that came the sound of urgent footsteps on stone, and in a few moments several of the Athenians appeared round a bend in the maze. After a moment of disbelief, they darted forward and took Theseus from Tilly and Oskar. Together they returned to the portcullis, where one of the young men shook the metal bars and called for the soldiers.

"Come quick! The Minotaur is defeated!" he called.

"It is no good," said a young woman despairingly. "It makes no matter. Minos will leave us here regardless."

"No," breathed Theseus as one of the men tried his best to tend to the wounds with bandages ripped from his robes. "He will need to see for himself what has happened to the Minotaur and his beloved labyrinth." And, true to Theseus's words, before long two soldiers emerged cautiously down the stairs.

"What's going on?" one of them said. "We can't let you out."

"What if we told you that Theseus has defeated the Minotaur?" the young man at the gate said, and they brought Theseus to show the soldier.

"It is true," Theseus said, breathless from pain. "It was a hard-won battle, but it is done."

"That is impossible," the soldier said. "Even if you had managed such a feat, to find your way back here is beyond mortal abilities."

"Perhaps the gods were on my side then," Theseus said, "and provided me with a path through the darkness."

"I'm not going to be the one telling the king about this," one soldier said.

"Oh no, nor me!" the other said.

"Well, one of you must," Tilly said sternly. "And Theseus needs a doctor." They looked blank. "A . . . um . . . physician?" she said, trying to find the word that would mean the right thing to them.

"I certainly do not think King Minos cares about healing anyone," the first soldier said. "He will care only for proof of what you claim has taken place."

"Either way, you need to take Theseus to Minos," Oskar said. "He's the only one who can tell the king what happened."

"Very well," the soldier said reluctantly. "As you say, there seems to be no other option."

He pulled on the great chain, raising the portcullis, and the group of Athenians staggered out of the deadly labyrinth. Color was already returning to Theseus's cheeks at the thought of his success. Tilly and Oskar followed the group up the steps and along to the entrance to the throne room, where Tilly spotted Ariadne anxiously waiting. But, as Theseus staggered forward to tell his tale to King Minos, Calliope appeared behind them.

"Come," she said. "You have done well. But you have another place to visit."

"I don't understand what we were supposed to learn here," Tilly said, exhausted. "If there was something we were meant to have found in the labyrinth, then we failed."

"You have found your way through," was all Calliope said before the grandeur of the Cretan court faded away.

Tilly and Oskar found themselves alone and outside, as snow fell around them. There was none of the ethereal beauty of Mount Olympus, nor any of the ostentatious riches of Minos's court. It was simply a field in winter. Tilly was glad of the woolen clothes they were wearing thanks to Bess, but they could not keep the cold out entirely.

"What do you think we should do?" she asked Oskar. "Do we wait for something to happen, or should we make our way toward those houses on the other side of the fields?"

"We may as well start that way," Oskar said. "But I imagine something will happen before we get there. Whether we like it or not."

# 28

## No Eating or Drinking

**O**skar was right. They had only gone a few paces before a wailing woman burst from a clump of trees.

"He has taken my daughter!" she cried. "And the Fates say that she may only return if she has not eaten of his food." She fell to the frozen ground in front of them, head in her hands. Tilly knelt beside her and put a gentle hand on her arm.

"Can we do anything to help?" she asked tentatively.

"We can only hope that he has not given her food or drink," the woman replied. She looked up at them properly for the first time. "And you are merely mortal children. You are kind to offer help, but you can do nothing—for there is no way for you to venture into Hades's kingdom."

"Hades . . ." Oskar repeated. "As in god of the Underworld Hades?"

"The same," the woman said. "He stole away my daughter, Persephone, to make her queen of his domain. I have spent many months searching for her, ignoring my duties, until the water whispered to me where she had been taken."

"What are your duties?" Tilly asked, and the woman gestured around them.

"Everything you can see," she said despondently. "I am Demeter, the goddess of agriculture, among other things. And in my neglect, the world has turned to snow and ice. But I must search for Persephone. I cannot care for the world until I know she is safe."

Tilly was trying to remember what she knew about the myth of Hades and Persephone. The "no eating or drinking" thing was familiar to her, but she couldn't remember the particulars.

"We might be able to find a way to your daughter," she offered.

"There is none," Demeter said. "When I told him of the Fates' decree, Zeus sent Hermes, the fastest of the gods, to see what Hades had done. I would that he had sent another, one less known for trickery and mischief, but Hermes is the one who knows the way. I cannot venture there alone, and neither can you."

"We're happy to give it a go," Oskar said. "We've got a few tricks up our sleeves." Demeter looked in confusion at Oskar's tunic. "Oh sorry," he said. "Nothing up my literal sleeves. I just mean there's a bit more to us than meets the eye. We have some friends in high places."

"You are watched over by one of the gods?" Demeter said, her curiosity piqued.

Oskar looked at Tilly, who wasn't sure how to respond. Calliope hadn't said whether or not they could tell others about why they were here.

"A goddess," Tilly answered slowly. "Calliope sent us on a journey."

"Why, then there is hope!" Demeter said, standing up. "If the goddess of epic poetry is directing your steps, then perhaps there is a chance for Persephone still. Calliope does sometimes welcome a happy ending. Once in a while. If you are willing to try and find a path to the kingdom of Hades, I would be at your and Calliope's mercy. Shall I call on her now?"

"Best not," Tilly said. "I'm not sure whether we were supposed to tell anyone she sent us here."

"I swear to keep it to myself," Demeter said. "But make haste if you do intend to go beneath, for time is short if we are to reach them before Hades has tricked my daughter into taking food or drink. Perhaps Calliope sent you into my path to align our purposes."

"Perhaps," Tilly said. "So, do you know how to get to the Underworld without having to actually die? We're keen to avoid that."

"It is Hermes who leads the souls of the dead to the River Styx," Demeter said. "And Charon who rows them across. It is not a journey for mortals, though, and I do not know what price

Charon will ask of you. But, if you hurry, you may still be able to follow Hermes, for Zeus only tasked him to go moments before we met. I will take you to where Hermes leads the dead. There are other secret routes, but they will take you too long and be too perilous."

Demeter took them by the hand and started walking. The *frozen fields seem to speed by,* turning to blurs of glimmering white under their feet. They covered huge amounts of space more quickly than any mortal could. Within seconds, they had arrived at a cavernous black opening in a cliff face surrounded by black poplar trees. They could just see a flicker of gold deep within the cave.

"Hermes!" Demeter shouted. "I do not wish you to tarry long, but there are two young souls who must go with you."

The gold flickering paused and then moved toward them. The gloom gradually revealed a slender, golden-haired man wearing sandals with flicking golden wings holding him a little way off the ground. He looked at Tilly and Oskar and laughed.

"Demeter," Hermes said, "I do not know what you think these two living children will achieve that I cannot."

"I do not trust you, Hermes," Demeter said, earning another laugh from Hermes.

"I care not for your trust or lack of it," he replied. "But it is not up to you whether I take these two down below. Charon will not accept them—you know that. He can only row the dead across the river."

"We can pay," Oskar said firmly.

"I assure you, you do not have the correct currency," Hermes replied.

"They were sent to me by Calliope," Demeter said, immediately breaking her promise to Tilly to keep that secret. Hermes looked at them with more interest.

"What does Calliope want with you?" he said, settling onto the ground. "Does Zeus know? Do the Fates?"

"There is no time to argue about such things," Demeter said. "Persephone has been down there for six months. You must complete the task Zeus has set for you, to go and see if she can be returned to me."

"That is not my task," Hermes reminded her. "It is to see if your daughter has eaten food or taken drink while she is there, as the Fates have decreed. For I will only bring her back if she has not. And my task is certainly not to take these two with me."

"We're probably just going to follow you anyway," Oskar said, and Hermes laughed once more.

"You would not be able to keep pace," he said.

"Try us," said Tilly, not at all sure that they could.

And with that taunt, Hermes gave a mischievous grin, whirled into the air, and was gone into the darkness with a flicker of his winged sandals.

"Uh, Tilly, we always trust each other, obviously, but I'm not sure how you thought that was going to work out," Oskar said quietly.

"I can imagine us there," Tilly said. "I'm sure I can. Hold on."

Oskar took her hand without question, and Tilly closed her eyes. She tried to draw together what Demeter and Hermes had told her, the half-formed images she could gather from books of myths she'd read or had read to her over the years. And she added in her own idea of what the Underworld might be like, summoning the sadness of loss, feeling it wash over her. Then there! The moment, the click into place, the alignment she was learning to look for that meant her imagination was in gear. And once she'd found it, they were gone from the mouth of the cave.

They emerged by the banks of a slowly moving river, standing on a small wooden pier that looked not far from crumbling into the dark waters beneath it. Seconds after they arrived, Hermes flew into view. He clapped in delight when he saw them, and Tilly couldn't help but feel quite satisfied, both at having imagined them successfully to the right place and at besting the mischievous god.

"You have surprised me, I will happily admit it," he said. "Has Calliope bestowed some of her powers on you?"

"Some," Tilly said. "But those were our own."

"Perhaps you will have something to bargain with then," Hermes replied, peering into the gloom.

A splashing could soon be heard, and a rickety wooden boat appeared, drawing up to the pier. Only one occupant sat aboard, the rower himself, who was dressed in black hooded robes. A pale hand reached out and secured the boat to the pier before the hood was pulled down. Underneath was a pale and haggard face, one that had not seen the sun for a very long time.

"What is this, Hermes?" Charon croaked. "They live still."

"They do," Hermes said. "I do not vouch for them, but they are no mere mortals who have accidentally wandered this way. Demeter brought them to me, and they have been touched by Calliope in some way. They have powers that no mortals should possess. I thought you might find them a curiosity if nothing else. I, however, am sent by Zeus to find Persephone—has she passed this way?"

"She did not come in my boat," Charon said. "For the Lord of the Underworld brought her himself, by his own route. But I saw them pass by. So. Her mother has learned of where she was taken. It was inevitable she would discover the truth eventually."

"She has," Hermes affirmed. "Demeter has neglected the earth itself in her search for her daughter. The world is cold and infertile while she seeks Persephone. The Fates have decreed that if the girl has not eaten or drunk, she will be freed, and Zeus has sent me to discover how the die will be cast. And if you allow these two to travel with you, I may come this slower way also, for I am curious as to what they might offer you and what they will do if they reach their destination."

"Very well," Charon said, looking up at Tilly and Oskar from the boat. "What do you offer instead of my usual fee? It is only those who have achieved great heroic acts who have ever ridden with me while still alive. Are you heroes?"

Tilly and Oskar looked at each other.

"How would you define a hero exactly?" Oskar asked. Charon looked stunned, and Hermes gave a smirk.

"A hero is one who has . . . done great deeds," Charon said. "Who has overcome adversity, who has been blessed by Mount Olympus, who has performed incredible tasks."

"Then, yeah," Oskar said simply. "I think we're heroes."

"We've definitely defeated some pretty dangerous people," Tilly said, remembering Enoch Chalk and the Underwood

twins, hoping that she would soon be able to add the Alchemist to that list. "And we've pulled off some pretty unlikely stunts, actually, things people said weren't possible. We've found hidden libraries, followed ancient maps, and mastered magic, and Calliope herself has helped us on this journey. So I think that ticks off most of your list."

Charon had clearly never dealt with anyone quite like Tilly and Oskar before.

"That may be," he said, "but the quality that sets heroes apart from all others is that their aims are noble and pure. What is your goal? Why do you seek to go where mortals cannot? It is more than aiding Demeter; I can sense that."

"Yes," Tilly said. "We are trying to save one of the most important things of all—imagination. Stories. Book magic. The things passed down from generation to generation. Why you live on here, and why we can come here at all. The glue that holds the world together."

"In that case," Charon said, "you may accompany me. I am content that you are heroes, even if you do not look like those I have encountered before."

"Thank you," Tilly said, and stepped down into the boat, Oskar right behind her.

"An impressive performance," Hermes said as he floated above them.

"It was all true," said Tilly.

"Just because something is a performance does not mean it

is not true," Hermes said. "I can see you know what you're doing when it comes to telling a story."

"Is that a compliment?" Tilly asked, unsure of where Hermes's allegiances lay.

"Of course," Hermes said. "What is a good life but a story well told?"

And with that, they were off. Charon lifted his oars, and the group made their way down the lapping black waters of the River Styx toward the Underworld and its king.

# 29

## Mortal Rules Do Not Apply

"Can I speed things along a little?" Hermes said after only a few minutes on the sluggish river.

"It is not how things are done," Charon replied, but Tilly noticed that Hermes quietly stuck his hand into the river anyway, and the boat started to speed along at a much greater rate. If Charon noticed too, he did not comment. With Hermes's help, it didn't take long to make their way through the dripping caverns. No light could be seen apart from the pale glow from the lamp at the front of the boat, and the flicker from Hermes's sandals.

As they slowed and drew up to another pier, Charon put his finger to his lips, although the darkness meant that Tilly and Oskar could not immediately see why.

Hermes, however, had no care for Charon's instructions, and nimbly hopped out of the boat and yawned before calling out, "Uncle Hades! Show yourself, you rogue! I come on Zeus's business!"

Charon shook his head and gestured for Tilly and Oskar to disembark. When Tilly stepped from the boat, there was an unsettling sound of scrabbling on rocks and a low growl. As Charon turned his boat around, a fearsome sight emerged from the depths of the shadows.

"Not another monster," Oskar groaned as Charon rowed silently away.

What they saw was truly monstrous: a gigantic three-headed dog that growled and slavered from high above them. Hermes, however, didn't seem particularly bothered.

"Uncle! Please call your hound off—it is your nephew Hermes!" he shouted into the gloom. He turned to Tilly and Oskar. "Usually, Cerberus—that's the dog—would eat you, given that you are alive, but do not worry. He obeys me. Most of the time."

"Most of the time?" Oskar repeated anxiously, edging as far away from Cerberus's greedy mouths as he could without falling into the Styx.

"And I bring two curiosities with me!" Hermes called into the darkness. He turned to Tilly and Oskar. "Probably best not announce why I am really here. I do not think Hades will take kindly to the Fates or Zeus involving themselves in his romantic endeavors."

"But he kidnapped Persephone, right?" said Tilly.

She remembered Merlin's tale about Arthur's birth and couldn't help but think that there were a lot of women in myths and legends whose sides of the story she would be keen to hear. She'd have to have a look in Pages & Co. after all this was over and see if anyone had written any books about it.

"It would seem so," Hermes replied, giving the three-headed dog a stern look as it approached.

"So shouldn't it be Persephone's choice whether she stays?" Tilly asked.

"Unfortunately, that is not quite how it works here," said Hermes.

"Hmmm." Tilly made her disapproval clear on her face.

Hermes looked unaffected. He produced a huge steak from somewhere Tilly could not make any sense of and tossed it to the dog, who immediately got distracted, its three heads fighting over the piece of meat, tiny between its giant jaws.

"Did you say that Hades was your uncle?" Oskar asked.

"Yes," said Hermes. "But our family tree is pretty complicated, and mortal rules do not apply. For example, Athena was born from Zeus's forehead, fully formed, in a suit of armor."

"Huh?" said Oskar, but Hermes was saved from having to explain by Cerberus's heads stopping fighting over the steak and lying whimpering on the ground. From behind the beast stalked a tall man wearing a robe of black. His skin was bone white, and his eyes glittered like onyxes in the darkness.

"Hermes," he said in a silky-smooth voice. "I hear you have come to meet my new bride."

"In a manner of speaking," Hermes said. "Zeus asked me to, you know, check in. Make sure she was doing okay."

"Of course," Hades said. "Do follow me—we were just sitting down to dinner."

# 30

## For Every Winter, There Must Be a Spring

"And who are you?" Hades asked Tilly and Oskar as they walked down a long corridor hewn from the shining black rock. "Do you also come to see how Persephone fares?"

"Sort of," Tilly said, wishing her nervousness was less evident in her voice. "We did want to help with that if we could, but we're also just . . . just . . ." She tailed off, not quite sure how to explain or whether she should even try.

"You are clearly very much alive," Hades said, taking a step toward them. "It does not take the god of death to see that. But there is something even stranger. There is an . . . essence, an energy about you that I cannot place. You are almost *too* alive—not a problem I encounter very frequently as I'm sure you can imagine. Where do you come from?"

"Earth?" Oskar hazarded.

"Well, yes, you are clearly not gods," Hades said dismissively.

"But . . . what is it I can sense?" He was clearly frustrated that he couldn't immediately work it out.

"Calliope is protecting them," Hermes answered for them. "Is that it?"

"Yes, perhaps a part of the answer," Hades said, looking at Tilly and Oskar with even more interest. "But there is something not of Earth or Mount Olympus. It is as if you are travelers from a . . . from a dream."

Tilly shrugged, not sure what else to do or say.

"Can we . . . can we come in?" she went with in the end, which provoked a short, sharp bark of laughter from Hades.

"Why, yes," he said. "Do be sure to wipe your sandals before you enter. I will spare you the sight of the rest of my arrivals and the cheerless Asphodel Fields. I could show you the happier plains of Elysium, but you might be tempted never to return home." He gave an icy smile, turned around, and stalked into the darkness. Hermes gestured that they should follow.

There was a moment of complete, annihilating dark, and then they emerged into a banquet hall built of black marble. A long table piled with decadent food ran down its center: roast birds, platters of fruit and vegetables, bottles of wine, many-tiered cakes, everything you could imagine. But the only person there was a rather bored-looking young woman, also wearing a black robe. She glanced up as the new arrivals entered, and an expression of wary relief crossed her face.

"Hermes?" she said, standing up. "Has my mother sent you?"

"Zeus," he said. "But yes, at the appeal of your mother."

"Have you come to take me home?" Persephone asked, running over to him.

"Uh, hopefully," Hermes said awkwardly. "The Fates are aware of the situation and have . . . stipulations."

"Of course they have," Persephone said, visibly wilting.

"The Fates have decreed that you may return home if you have not eaten or drunk in Hades's kingdom," Hermes said, looking uncomfortably at the feast.

"Oh, then I am free to go!" Persephone said. "I have refused all food and drink since I arrived."

"That is not quite so, dearest," Hades said, and walked over to them, holding a black platter. On it was a single broken-open pomegranate.

"I didn't eat that," Persephone said, but Tilly could see the doubt on her face.

"Oh, but you did," Hades insisted. "You ate six seeds from this pomegranate. My orchardist bore witness. Come, Ascalaphus." A man emerged from the shadows, looking uncertain. "Did Persephone eat six seeds from this fruit?" Hades asked.

"Yes," Ascalaphus said quietly in a curious hooting voice. "I saw her walking in the gardens, pluck one of the pomegranates, break it open, and eat its seeds."

"A shame, dear Persephone," Hades said, "but those are the rules that have been set. And who are we to argue with the Fates?"

"I will tell them what I have seen," Hermes said, and with no further explanation or good-bye, he took to his heels and flew away, leaving Tilly and Oskar with Hades and Persephone.

"If we eat your food, do we have to stay here too?" Oskar asked. "Because I am starving."

"I shall permit you not to be bound by such rules," Hades said. "As nothing of your nature fits here or above, I do not wish to have to work out what to do with you or where to put you—so eat. Hermes will not be long—he has ways of traveling that are faster when he is on his own. Come, join me."

Tilly could not quite believe that Oskar was willing to risk it, and tried to communicate that with her eyes, but he just shrugged and started assembling a sandwich. Persephone looked on enviously.

"Will you tell me more of what you are seeking?" Hades asked, sitting on a throne of ornately carved black stone at the head of the table. "Or why Calliope the Muse has taken an interest in you?"

"We were told that she had answers that could help us," Tilly said, very wary of telling Hades anything.

"About what?" he pressed.

"About a problem we're trying to solve," she said.

Hades laughed. "I see you are keen to keep your secrets! I thought perhaps I could assist you."

"I don't think so," Tilly said, trying to sound polite.

"I dunno," Oskar added as he spooned roasted potatoes

onto a plate. "Death probably actually does know quite a lot about stories."

"Stories, you say?" Hades said, eyes lighting up. "Why, of course I do. All of us on or below Mount Olympus are fueled by the stories that others tell about us. I would not have such power if people were not so fascinated by me."

"So people telling stories about you makes you more powerful?" asked Tilly.

"Oh, of course. It is why you have probably heard of me, but never one of those ridiculous minor gods who will choose hunting over an adventure, or a nymph who prefers swimming to great or terrible deeds. No one cares for them, and so they do not endure as I do. Most stories and histories are lost to time or war."

Tilly felt like she should be taking something from what he said, but it felt just out of reach. These journeys were like being given jigsaw pieces but never from the same puzzle. But maybe she just needed a picture to follow.

Before she could ask Hades more, Hermes returned in a flicker of golden feathers.

"A plot twist!" he said with a mischievous smile on his face. Hades and Persephone both looked uncertain. "One that perhaps will not be satisfying to either of you, or—who knows?— perhaps a welcome compromise. The Fates have decreed that Persephone will stay in the Underworld as queen for six months of the year for the six seeds that she ate in Hades's realm. For the other six months, she may return to the land of the living. How does that suit you both?"

Hades and Persephone looked at each other, and to Tilly's surprise, they shrugged and shook hands.

"You're okay with that?" Tilly said.

"It seems fair," Persephone said.

"As I told you," Hermes said under his breath, "things work differently here." To Persephone, he put his hand out. "My lady, you have been here six months, and so may I accompany you to a sunnier climate?"

Persephone and Hermes linked arms and walked back toward the cave. Hades looked similarly unfazed.

"I shall see you in six months!" he called, picking up an apple and biting into it. "And you two," he said to Tilly and Oskar, "I will not detain; you will need to keep up with Hermes to get back out and past Cerberus. But here is something to ponder as you return to the land of the living. Remember what endures. We may all be rulers of our own realm, but it does not mean that we know what happens next."

"That's . . . extremely cryptic," Oskar said, grabbing a loaf of bread for the road.

"Best be off," Hades said, sauntering away. "I hear Hermes's wings afluttering."

Tilly and Oskar did not have much choice and ran after Hermes.

"Must I take you all?" he grumbled. "Fine, fine—hold firm."

He gathered Persephone and the two bookwanderers to him, and with a *gust of air* and a flicker of feathers, a bright light burst from him, obliterating the dark walls of the Underworld from view. When the light faded, they were standing outside, in the very spot they had first met Demeter. But the land was no longer snowy and barren but luscious and green. Trees were fluffy with blossom, and wildflowers grew around their feet. The sound of laughter and music was on the breeze, which smelled of honey and roses. Tilly could barely believe it was the same place. Then a shriek of joy pierced the tranquility, and Demeter was running toward them through the meadow. Persephone flung herself into her mother's arms, and they both wept with joy.

"See, a happy ending," Hermes said. "For now. If you can endure the winter and her snows, then spring and her blossoms will always come back round again."

"Indeed, for every winter, there must be a spring," said a voice behind them, and there was Calliope. "Thank you, Hermes. Now, Tilly, Oskar. You have seen the three things I asked you to, but we have one final destination, where we will be able to speak finally after all you have seen. There are three more people to meet. Their names are Clotho, Lachesis, and Atropos, but you will have heard them called the Fates."

# 31

## How Long Is a Piece of Thread?

With a gentle hand on each of their shoulders, Calliope once more guided Tilly and Oskar through mythology. Their destination proved to be a great hall that looked disconcertingly like the Archive before it had started to decay. Shelves and shelves of bound books towered above them, but unlike the bright white tomes of the Archive, these books were made of brass and iron, and rested on shelves of stone. Otherworldly light shone down from above, golden and mottled like a permanent sunset.

"These are the archives of the Fates," Calliope explained. "They hold destinies in their hands and possess power even Zeus does not, though he wishes otherwise. Would you like to meet them?"

"It was them that said Persephone had to stay in the Underworld for six months if she'd eaten anything," Tilly pointed out nervously.

"They will permit you to ask about that if you wish," Calliope replied. "They have answers to many of your questions, and I promise they are no threat to you. Come."

She led them out of the library to a circular room lit by many, many candles tucked into alcoves. The only other furniture in the room was a wooden spindle at its center and three stools. Sitting on the stools were three elderly women in robes of black. The one in the middle was spinning, while the woman to her right held a wooden rod and measured the thread against it as it was produced. The last snipped the thread decisively with a pair of shears. Each length of thread was different, but the women consulted no lists of notes, just spun and measured and snipped.

As the visitors walked toward them, the spindle slowed, and the three Fates looked silently up at them.

They were older than anyone Tilly had ever seen before, with shining white hair and bright black eyes. Their faces were stern but not frightening.

"Calliope," the spinner said in a voice that sounded clear and young.

"Clotho," Calliope replied, nodding her head in respect. "I bring two travelers to speak with you. Tilly, Oskar, Clotho and her sisters look after the past, the present, and the future between them. Our destinies are all in their hands."

"What do you wish to speak with us about?" Clotho asked, looking at Tilly. "This is a sacred place, and you are mortal. Although you have something . . . eternal about you."

"Tilly and Oskar are two young bookwanderers," Calliope said, but at the word "bookwanderers," the three Fates hissed in displeasure.

"They are not welcome here," the measurer said. "Not since the great theft."

"I know our history, Lachesis," Calliope replied.

"Then you must have a purpose in bringing them to us," the cutter said, standing and coming closer.

"I do, Atropos," said Calliope. "They came to me in search of aid and in search of knowledge, and I never refuse a request for more understanding. They do not know of the theft; I do not believe any of those who currently call themselves bookwanderers do. And I think that it is finally time, with these two, to set that right."

"What are you talking about?" Tilly said, feeling a tangle of anxiety deep in her bones. "What great theft?"

"We will tell you," Calliope said. "But first I ask a little more patience. To ensure that you understand what I have to share with you, I need to know that you have learned what you must from the places I sent you."

Tilly felt very stressed; she hated feeling like she didn't know what was happening or that she didn't understand what was expected of her.

"I'm not sure we got anything specific," Oskar said, trying to help. "We met your mother, who was lovely, and she obviously told us about the importance of knowing what came before us." And it was the way that Oskar phrased it, and where they were standing when he did, that helped Tilly finally see the picture she had been given all the pieces for.

"And we went through the labyrinth," she said slowly, trying to get her words to catch up with her brain. "We just kept going, following the thread. And then we went to the Underworld and back . . . and learned that spring will always follow winter. The past, the present, and the future. It's what stories show us, right? Why they're so important and hold everything together?"

Calliope gave her a smile that was so warm and so proud that Tilly would remember it for the rest of her life.

"Who we were, who we are, and who we hope to be," Calliope said. "Stories show us where we came from—the lives of people before us, their hopes, their failings, their dreams. But not everyone's stories are remembered, and even this speaks to our history—what we value, what we protect, and who we let tell our stories. There are so many stories that are lost to time or to injustice. It is in our power, though, to help choose which stories remain. And in the present, books are a thread to follow, a way to reflect and understand and grow. They allow us to escape and roam and learn beyond our own limits and experiences, to think about who we are and what we stand for, and to find our way back again. And finally . . ."

"Stories help us decide who we want to be," Tilly said, remembering the words her grandad had said to her almost a year ago, before she even knew she was a bookwanderer.

"Precisely," Calliope said. "The yarns that come before us are what we weave our worlds from. They offer a way to imagine the world differently and help us set a path to get there."

"I don't mean to be rude," Oskar said quietly, "but I don't really understand what all this has to do with stopping the Alchemist."

"There are limits as to how much I can help you with him, as I cannot see him or his actions clearly, only feel their impact," Calliope said.

"Can you come with us?" Tilly asked. "Sometimes I can bring people from books with my bookwandering magic!"

"I cannot," Calliope said. "My powers are greatly diminished in your world. But also you have come via another liminal space, some secret corner of Story, one I cannot go to. It must be a reader who stops him, someone mortal."

There was the sound of the spindle whirring again, and Clotho spoke as she worked.

"Human lives run in lines," she said as her sisters held the thread against a rod and snipped it. Atropos held it up in a shimmering streak.

"They have beginnings and ends," she said. "The fact that a life must end gives it great power, a potent magic all its own. The freedom to do what you choose with the thread that is allotted to you."

"You may tell a tale of great adventure or one of quiet purpose, and both have equal value," Lachesis said, measuring a new thread against her rod. "And hopefully, when the thread is run out, you will look back and say that was a life well told, and I am content for my book to be returned to the great library of the Fates."

"But stories are circles," Clotho went on, gesturing at her wheel as it spun round and round. "They are made from the same stuff as life but formed in a different shape. And in stories great power comes from the fact that an ending is always also a beginning."

"We went to see Persephone . . ." Tilly started, but hesitated, intimidated.

"You do not think it just, what we decreed?" Lachesis asked.

"Well, I just wondered why, if she didn't want to stay, that you said she had to," Tilly said.

"Lines and circles," Clotho replied with the first smile the Fates had offered. "Persephone is a circle, one that will loop and loop, spring to winter and round again. You do understand this already, deep inside, or you would not have been brought here."

"Can we . . . see our own threads?" Oskar asked tentatively.

"No," Lachesis said. "But you knew that also. The magic of a human thread would be diminished by knowing how long it was."

Oskar nodded.

"Now you understand why it must be you who return and stop this," Calliope said. "But before you leave, I hope that I will be able to furnish you with what you need to disentangle this man from the world's imagination. If what you say is true, he has managed to connect himself to its power in a deep and profound way, and to stretch his thread far longer than the Fates had cut it. You must find a way to reverse these things. This Alchemist you speak of is clearly a real and dangerous threat. But if you wish to stop him, and to stop someone like him from rising again, there is an even greater threat you must defeat. The architect of the great theft. The one who stole from us and from the other guardians, and codified and bound what he took and turned it into rules and regulations and punishments in order to control it. The Fates are repelled by the word 'bookwandering' because that is the term he gave that magic when he bound it in a book of rules and made all readers subject to them."

"Who?" Tilly asked, although she realized that she already knew what Calliope was going to say.

"His name is Merlin," Calliope replied. "The first bookwanderer, the thief."

# 32

## A Rare Gift

There was a moment of horrible silence as Tilly and Oskar took in the information.

"So . . . Merlin, what, stole imagination from you?" Oskar asked. "Bookwandering isn't as old as imagination?"

"Certainly not as you understand it," Lachesis said bitterly.

"Stories are protected by all who read them, all who write them, and all they tell of," explained Clotho. "There are very few older than us who remain, but it is the task of all readers to preserve and protect imagination. So that any reader can bookwander, can write the stories of their lives and dreams, can wonder without limits. It is not in the nature of imagination to be bound and ruled over, siphoned off for selfish causes or used to prolong the mortal life of individuals."

"But . . . Merlin can't access the real world," Tilly said. "He's a circle, not a line."

"Merlin is crafty and clever and took control of the magic

of stories a very long time ago," Calliope explained. "The rules he created to control it were written into a book of great power, which he tried to hide from everyone. But it could not be entirely controlled because he is not human as you are. As you say, he is a circle, and so there has always been one reader in every generation who could penetrate his defenses, one who knew stories in their bones."

"Good old Milo," Oskar said affectionately.

"So he was lying when he said he had created that system to protect the Book?" Tilly asked.

"Yes," Atropos confirmed.

"And he used this stolen magic he had taken to carve out an eternal layer for himself," Calliope went on. "To direct events from inside Story as much as he was able to. He has had undue and unearned influence on which stories lasted, on the way the world understands magic—and power. He may not be able to physically access your world, but he has found ways of spying on it. There was a bookwanderer a long time ago who stumbled across Merlin in his hiding place, and the wizard convinced him to create an equivalent pocket and hide away there. Merlin gave instructions on how to make an archive of sorts—the idea stolen from the Fates. And through that place Merlin found a way to observe the journeys of bookwanderers."

"Are you talking about the Archive?" Tilly said in shock. "But we've been there! It was destroyed! And Artemis, who looked after it, never said anything about Merlin."

"She may have never known he was behind it," Calliope said. "Merlin used that bookwanderer to keep his influence hidden. I am happy to hear it was destroyed. That will have been a great blow to Merlin."

"But it was a good place," Tilly said disconsolately. "We were sent there to get help, and the Archivists were great writers like Shakespeare—he helped us too!"

"It sounds as though the Archive grew beyond Merlin's reach," Calliope said with some satisfaction. "Imagination has fought back against him, spilled from the constraints he made. And also perhaps that there were people whose desire to help and guide overrode Merlin's intentions."

"But, hang on, does that mean Merlin already knew about the Alchemist?" Oskar asked in horror.

"I think it is likely," Calliope said. "It sounds like you know more than me of how the Archive came to be, but I doubt any bookwanderer of great power would have evaded his notice. There is no way he could keep his eyes on the lives of all bookwanderers, but anomalies would stand out to him. The Alchemist, however, knows either very little or none of this, otherwise he would not be searching for the Book. It creates limits and boundaries, and it seems that he seeks the opposite."

"So the Book is a . . . bad thing?" Tilly said, deflated. "After all we've gone through to find it? And does that mean all the Underlibraries, all of that, it's all Merlin?"

"I do not know much of these Underlibraries," Calliope

said. "You must remember that my sisters and I reside in myth and story, just like Merlin. We cannot clearly see what happens in your world and time; only the Fates can penetrate that veil. But Merlin bent the magic to his will, and mortals will have created more layers of rules—as they are wont to do. Some will have done it in good faith to protect their fellow readers and stories, and some will have done it to preserve power and access. I cannot tell you which rules were created by Merlin and which by your fellow bookwanderers. But the Book is not bad in itself: it is a vessel, as all books are. But it is how Merlin's magic is preserved."

Tilly felt as though she were standing on the deck of a boat rocked by vast waves. Everything she knew about bookwandering was shifting under her feet, but there was something in the pit of her stomach that was unsurprised that this was how it had come to be. It was the instinct that had led her to free the Source Editions at the British Library, and the confusion around why her mother had been punished for breaking the bookwandering rules.

"This is why Merlin is able to use imagination so freely then?" she asked. "Because he didn't bind himself to the bookwandering rules he created?"

"I doubt he would limit himself so," said Calliope.

"He shouldn't have showed us that we could do it too if we tried," Tilly said, her brain racing at how to use that to defeat him. "But does that mean the rules are real or not?"

"All rules can be broken," Calliope answered. "The difficult thing is to understand which should be."

Everything had changed, but somehow everything made sense, Tilly thought. But what to do about it?

"Do we need to destroy the Book?" Tilly asked.

"I think that would be a good start," Calliope replied. "Or perhaps a good ending. Are you ready to return?"

"I think so," Tilly said nervously, checking with Oskar, who nodded. "Unless there's anything more you can help us with?"

"You have it within you already," Calliope said. "You already did. I just showed you the shape of it, and gave you one end of a thread to follow through the labyrinth. It is up to you to bring spring back."

"Beautifully said, dear Calliope," Atropos said, holding her shears at her side as she moved toward them. "But I think there is something we can give you two that may be of more practical use. Come with me."

They followed Atropos back through the library of the Fates until she found what she was looking for. She pulled down a brass-and-iron volume and held it out to them.

"This is a rare gift," she said. "For my sisters and me to put the fate of another into the hands of two mortal children is a story you will never read again. But here is one tale that needs its ending changed."

Tilly took the book and opened its cover to see Greek letters she couldn't understand.

"Apologies," Atropos said with a smile, and waved her hand over its pages so that the letters slid into English. They spelled: "Geronimo della Porta."

"It's like his Record," Oskar breathed.

"It is more than a Record, it is his life itself," Atropos said. "It has been spun and measured, but it cannot be severed by us. Take it with you, for his fate is now in your hands."

"It is time for you to go now," Calliope said, and kissed each of them on the forehead.

Tilly felt terrified, hopeful, and overwhelmed all at the same time. She and Oskar linked arms, and she imagined Bess's tavern as clearly as she could. There was a fizz and a shimmer, but they didn't move, staying firmly in the Fates' library with Calliope, who gave a frown.

"Do you need further assistance?" she asked.

"Uh, I'm not sure," Tilly said. "We don't have the book to return from in the way we'd normally bookwander, because Merlin showed us, for some reason, that we didn't need one. But I can't seem to imagine us back like I did earlier. Oskar, you have a go. Just imagine Bess's, or maybe try the courtyard where the sword in the stone and the Book were."

Oskar closed his eyes, but there was only the same moment of shimmering air and then nothing.

"Merlin sent you here directly?" Calliope said, looking worried. "Why would he send you where he knows you would learn the truth?"

"I guess he doesn't care what we know if he's made sure we can't get back," Tilly said, feeling increasingly panicky. "Once Horatio told us we had to come and find you, there's no way he couldn't have helped us without giving everything away, and so he's obviously done something to stop us getting back. And the others will all be with him—and won't know what he's up to! Hang on, what does Rosa know?"

"Who is Rosa?" Calliope asked with a frown.

"She was supposed to be the guardian of *The Book of Books*," Tilly said. "Given what we know about that, though, I'm not sure what that means about her. But she is one of the nicest, bravest people I've ever met! She can't know the truth—I trust her. I think she's been hoodwinked along with the rest of us. Merlin has somehow convinced a line of book-wanderers that he's on our side, and they need to help him by stopping anyone else getting to the Book. She's been helping him without realizing. We really need to get back to Milo and Alessia."

Tilly sat down on the hard floor with a bump as she tried to make her brain work faster. Absentmindedly, she played with her bee necklace, the one that matched her mother's, and thought about the way that they had been able to find their way back to each other.

"The triskele!" she said, leaping to her feet. "Merlin gave me and Milo a triskele each, remember? He said they were siblings and that as long as they were both in Story, they would connect to each other. Milo and Alessia will be back by now, surely?"

"Or they'll still be in Norse mythology, and Merlin will be blocking them too," Oskar said.

"Alessia was clever, though," Tilly said in admiration. "As always. She insisted on taking Rosa's book. Merlin might have a way to block that, but it won't be the same. Plus, I bet he wants to know exactly where Milo is, given that he's the only other person who can access the Book."

"So how does the triskele work?" Calliope said, looking at the symbol with interest.

"Is it a *Wizard of Oz* sort of thing?" Oskar asked. "Like a click-your-heels-together thing? Maybe, like, rub it at the same time?"

"I can't tell if you're joking," Tilly said. "Perhaps we should just ask it? Hold on tight." Oskar took her hand again, and Tilly held the triskele firmly.

"Find your sibling," she said out loud, and then in her head, with as much conviction as she could muster, *please*.

And this time the shimmer rose and did not vanish

but gradually clouded the Fates and Calliope from view.

Tilly just saw Calliope give them a solemn nod before Olympus vanished for good, and they found themselves standing in the courtyard of the cathedral, where Milo and Alessia were trapped in the stone itself, as was . . .

"Grandad!" Tilly burst into tears and ran across to her silenced grandfather.

# 33

## We Just Need Some Practice

Tilly wrapped her arms around Archie, who hugged her back tightly to show that he was okay, despite the magic binding him. He clearly mouthed, *I love you.*

"Are the others okay?" she asked. "Grandma and Mum?" Archie nodded, and Tilly felt a tiny part of her relax slightly. "They're back at Pages & Co., safe?" Archie nodded again.

"Tilly, Oskar, we need to tell you something quickly," Alessia said. "It's Merlin. He's . . ."

"Bad, we know," Tilly said.

"How?"

"Calliope told us," Oskar said. "How did you find out?" Alessia gestured at her trapped legs.

"Oh right," Oskar said.

"Horatio's awake but can't speak either," Milo said, pointing to his uncle. "Do you also know that the Alchemist is here?"

"What?" Tilly said in horror.

"I guess we told Merlin everything he needed to know, so

he let the Alchemist through the gateway in Pages & Co. once we were all safely in our myths. I don't think they've been working together the whole time, though."

"No," Tilly confirmed, and as quickly as possible the four bookwanderers swapped all the information they had gathered.

After that, the immediate problem was the stone prisons most of them were caught in. Oskar gave the stone a kick, but that, predictably, didn't do anything.

"We need to use our imaginations," Tilly said firmly. "It's like what Hades said—we can all be rulers of our own realms, but it doesn't mean we know what happens next. This may be Merlin's realm, but he's the one who's showed us what we can do here because he didn't think he'd let us have the chance to use that against him."

"It's what Calliope said too," Oskar added. "We have what we need. We have our imaginations. Can we imagine our wooden swords into real ones, do you think?"

"Great idea," Alessia said. "We must imagine what we need, and then smash our way out."

She grabbed the wooden sword from her belt and held it up; the other three followed suit. It seemed so silly to be brandishing toy swords against the might of Merlin and the Alchemist, but it was what they had. Closing their eyes, the four of them imagined as hard as they could, and then, with a crackle and a shimmer, their swords were transformed.

"Oh," Tilly said in confusion as she opened her eyes.

She was no longer holding a wooden sword, but neither was she holding a real one. A quill, made of a white feather with a silver tip, was resting in her palm. And as she turned to look at the others, she saw none of them were holding swords either. The closest anyone had gotten was Oskar, who was grasping a huge hammer.

"That looks like Thor's," Milo pointed out.

"Honestly, that is low-key what I was imagining," Oskar admitted. "I was thinking about how a massive hammer would be way more useful to break these stones than a real sword, so I guess that's what I got."

"I certainly wasn't wishing for a quill," Tilly said in frustration.

"And I certainly wasn't wishing for this," Alessia said in disgust. It turned out she was holding a wooden sword still, but it had shrunk to the size of a crayon. And not only that but . . .

"Is it . . . growing?" asked Milo.

"It does seem to be," Alessia said, perturbed. The miniature wooden sword was sprouting tiny shoots, and within moments it was covered in miniature leaves and flowers.

"Right then," she said, red-faced as she put it in her pocket, "what did you get, Milo?"

Milo had been naively hoping that no one would ask him that, because his wooden sword had vanished and been replaced by nothing at all. He held out his empty hands, blushing.

"I guess my imagination knows I'd be pretty useless with a sword," he said bashfully. "I knew the vorpal sword in the Jabberwock poem was a fluke. It's no big deal." He couldn't even look at his uncle, imagining the expression of resigned disappointment that was no doubt on Horatio's face currently.

"We just need some practice," Oskar reassured him. "It's not like anyone actually managed to imagine themselves a proper sword." The two boys looked at Alessia and Tilly, who were examining the quill.

"At least you know what to do with what you imagined," Milo pointed out, gesturing at the stone encasing his feet.

"Oh right!" Oskar said. "Hope everyone trusts me!"

"I do trust you, Oskar," said Alessia solemnly. "But please be very careful."

Horatio and Archie looked considerably more nervous as Oskar picked up the hammer and swung it at Alessia's legs. Thankfully, he got the swing just right, and the stone keeping Alessia glued to the spot shattered cleanly, and she staggered free.

"Amazing," Oskar said, looking at the hammer. "It's like I knew just how hard to swing it to break the stone without hurting you."

"I guess it came straight from your imagination," Alessia replied, giving him a high five. Oskar freed Milo next, just as easily.

"So, what do we do once we've freed everyone?" Tilly

asked. "We need to destroy the Book to defeat Merlin, and we also need to untangle the Alchemist from imagination—and we have the book the Fates gave me, and we have the eitr. Can we just throw it on the book? And where have they taken *The Book of Books?*"

"So many important books," Oskar said, pausing to wipe his brow. "Someone should have come up with better names for them."

"It is book magic," Tilly pointed out. "There's going to be a lot of important books. But we need both of them, ideally without Merlin or the Alchemist realizing we're back."

"I am afraid it is too late for that," said Merlin, before giving a flick of his staff. The Alchemist's book of fate flew out of Tilly's hands and into Merlin's.

"I'll take that," the Alchemist said, holding his hand out, but Merlin ignored him. The Alchemist's expression turned stony, but he would not lose face in front of his enemies, especially when they were children and, worse, his daughter.

Oskar quickly tried to swing the hammer at the stone holding Archie, but this time he couldn't even pick it up from the ground.

"I think not," Merlin said. "Matilda and Oskar, welcome back," he went on. "I am curious to know how you got through the barriers locking access to my realm."

"You gave us the key," Tilly said, showing the triskele around her neck.

"A frustrating oversight on my part," Merlin said with a twitch of his brow. "But nevertheless you will see I have everything I need. As does my new . . . colleague. You all told me so many interesting things about this man you were working against, and I have felt his power for a long time. I thought that, on the whole, I would probably have more in common with him than with you."

"You're not wrong," Oskar muttered.

"Between us, we can truly take charge of the world's imagination," Merlin said. "Both here and in your world. Geronimo has managed quite extraordinary feats within the web of bookwandering laws I built. It honestly amazes me that it has taken quite so long for someone to realize how flexible they could be if you were truly looking for how to bend them. But people do love to follow rules and authority, don't they? Revolution does not come naturally to many. I have been hearing about your train, though, Milo—a rebellious spirit there, for sure."

"And you did all this to live forever, and to dictate the shape of imagination, and to control how people traveled in it, and . . . As I'm saying this out loud, it's actually super clear why you did it," Oskar said.

"And with Geronimo on board, I can move faster than ever, rather than carving out pieces of Story one chip at a time," Merlin said. "And keep readers occupied with the lovely set of rules I have created for them."

"But they are real in some way, aren't they?" Tilly said.

"Because I broke the rules by accident, and bookwandering definitely worked differently for me."

"Quite," Merlin said. "Do not think that it is a simple thing to circumvent them. Here it is a little easier because we are in pure Story, but in your world it takes a great deal of effort, understanding, and time to work out how to skirt around their edges. Those rules are very real for most bookwanderers, very real indeed. You are an anomaly, as there has been the odd anomaly before you. And, of course, I tried to get to you before, tried to reclaim you."

"It was you!" Tilly said. "You lied earlier!"

"Yes, of course I did," Merlin said dismissively. "What? Do you think I would tell you the truth? Yes, it was me trying to get you back into Story so I could remove you from the equation. I tried to keep track of you via my Archive, but its true purpose was distorted, and the whims of bookwanderers changed it. Even the guardian I created was warped by her ridiculous insistence on trying to help people. She did not know of me or where she had come from, and yet kept sending out her maps and taking care of bookwanderers! I did not expect the Archive to start drawing great writers to it, but initially I saw it as proof of my power, except that I could not keep it stable. And I learn now that it was you who destroyed it in the end!"

"Well, actually, it was already well on its way out," Tilly said. "Because the Underwoods were secretly destroying Source

Editions, so it was your own rules that ruined it. If you hadn't made it so that the Source Editions held so much power, then they wouldn't have been able to shake the foundations of your creepy spy library."

"Caught in a web of my own making," Merlin said. "Again. But with Geronimo, I can rebuild it if I wish. Now, on to more important matters. You four have meddled for long enough, and I grow bored of you. It is time for your stories to end."

# 34

## What Came to Mind

Tilly had come to recognize the twitch of Merlin's hand before he used his staff, and so, as soon as his fingers moved and without time to think it through properly, she imagined a tree. And, right in front of them, a great oak grew up from underneath Merlin and the Alchemist so fast that it caught them in its branches in awkward twists, pushing them high off the ground.

"Oh, I see, Matilda," Merlin said. "It is to be like this, is it? Very well." And with that, he jumped from the tree and floated down.

The Alchemist followed, slightly more uncertainly. Merlin lit Tilly's tree on fire with a flick, and standing in front of the burning trunk, he conjured a cage around them. Tilly tried but could not imagine the cage away and so quickly imagined a key for the lock and swung the door open.

"A lovely touch," Merlin said, before imagining a great wall of fire that swept out from the burning tree across the court-yard, separating Tilly and Alessia from Oskar and Milo.

"We can do this!" Tilly shouted to the others, steeling herself for battle. Alessia was the first to focus herself, and suddenly she was wearing a suit of armor. Unfortunately, clearly the only armor she had in her imagination was a very old-fashioned and heavy set, which she had to immediately imagine off again.

"I hope my father didn't see that," she said.

Meanwhile, Milo was focusing as hard as he could, and then *pop*—to his relief, he imagined two protective domes hovering over Horatio and Archie. Oskar realized that while Merlin's attention was focused on Tilly he could once again wield his hammer and quickly ran back over to Archie and held it up to ask permission. Archie nodded frantically, and Oskar gave the stone prison a whack, crumbling it to pieces. He quickly released Horatio next.

Merlin noticed and swore.

"Enough of that!" he said before a flick of his staff meant Oskar's hammer was once again too heavy to hold.

"Why can Merlin make that work," Alessia said in frustration, "when we can't affect what he creates? We can only imagine our own things, not change his!"

"Because I am manipulating the very air and molecules around you!" Merlin taunted. "Your grandfather and uncle are talking, but you cannot hear them! Just like I am not stopping Oskar from raising his hammer but rather affecting the gravity where the hammer is resting. Please remember: while you can hurl trees and suchlike at me, I have been studying imagination for longer than you have even been alive. This is my realm, and there are things I can do that you could not even dream of. You can try and protect yourselves as long as you have the energy, but you will tire, and then you will lose."

With a flourish of his staff, a great red dragon appeared in the sky, swooping down with fire belching from its open jaws.

Oskar quickly imagined protection, and they all ended up holding umbrellas that turned out to be fire-resistant.

"It's just what came to mind!" Oskar said.

"It works—that's all that matters!" Tilly shouted. "Amazing! Alessia, you and Milo focus on what your father is doing! Oskar and I will keep track of Merlin! Grandad, you come with us! Horatio, you stay with them! You can imagine anything here! You just need to believe you can!"

The battle raged on. There was no time to think of clever ways to stop the Alchemist and Merlin because every ounce of energy the others had was bound up in stopping the attacks thrown at them. They built walls of ice to stop fire, and sheets of fire to melt arrows of ice. Oskar even turned the floor to jelly at one point. "Just to see what would happen!" he shouted. And it did seem to profoundly irritate Merlin.

"Actually, Oskar, you've cracked it," said Tilly eagerly. "They're focused on violence and weapons; we need to think of the things they never could. It's back to what Hades was telling us—just because this is Merlin's realm, it doesn't mean he has control over what happens next! I'll concentrate on deflecting their attacks—you do whatever you can think of, the sillier the better!"

So, while Tilly made sure none of the Alchemist's or Merlin's fire or arrows or blades found purchase, Oskar succeeded in irritating and wrong-footing them at every turn through the pure joyfulness of his imagination. A hall of mirrors appeared, clattering down from the sky and trapping them in a maze of their own reflections. That shattered, Merlin and the Alchemist found themselves tangled in a web of Silly String while clown music played.

Despite how dangerous this battle was, Tilly almost had to laugh at the sight of them getting angrier and angrier as they were caught up in Oskar's carnival tricks. Alessia quickly realized what Oskar was doing and contributed her own imagination, which, of course, had its own flavor. Suddenly a maze of stone, not mirrors, sprang up, complete with booby traps and concealed dangers.

"How on earth did you imagine that all in one go?!" Oskar shouted in admiration, and Alessia got pink spots of pleasure on her cheeks as she added a manticore, with the body of a lion and the tail of a scorpion. Her next touch was an extremely unsettling echo effect whereby a horrifying shrieking noise whipped around the courtyard.

"Okay, that's bad for us all, Alessia!" Tilly shouted.

"Sorry, just experimenting!" Alessia called back before giving her head a flick and swapping the shrieking for a field of deadly nightshade. But her father was good at anticipating what she might do. Although he had taken no time to get to know her as she was growing up, she had learned from books and notes stolen from his desk, so he knew the way she thought—the same way he did. The field of poisonous plants had fire raining down on it within moments.

"Enough!" bellowed Merlin.

With a great whack of his staff to the ground, the burned flowers flew away to ash, and the strangest sensation rippled through the courtyard. It was as if the air itself were shaking, and Tilly immediately started feeling nauseous as her vision became distorted. Around them their defenses literally crumbled away: Alessia's maze of stone fell to rubble, and Oskar's mirrors shattered into fine pieces. The animals Alessia had conjured dissolved into nothingness, and even Oskar's jelly was shaken into submission, hardening into something granite-like. Once everything that had been imagined was gone or destroyed, the air stilled.

"Enough," Merlin repeated.

# 35

## The Last Bookwanderer

I will not endure your silly tricks," Merlin said, his voice ringing with venom. "It is time to end this charade. I have work to do. I assure you, if you try to repel anything further, your end will come swiftly and decisively. I have been playing, really, giving you a chance to see what I can do, but you are quick learners. I give you that much. Which means your stories must end here. You cannot be permitted to return to the real world and tell others of what you have learned, otherwise my power here will be stripped from me. Well, they will try, at least. But I would rather not risk that. I am sure you understand. Now, where is the other one? The so-called Anonymous Reader?"

Tilly looked around. She and Alessia were standing back-to-back, Grandad not far away. Oskar was only a little to their left, with Horatio at his side. Milo was nowhere to be seen. Tilly scanned desperately around to see if he was lying injured somewhere, but he had vanished entirely.

"Did you do something to him? Send him somewhere?" Alessia said angrily.

"No," said Merlin slowly. "He could have sent himself somewhere, of course. Run away to hide in a book to leave you all to fight."

"He would never do that," Alessia said, and Tilly knew she was right. But where was he?

There was a moment of stillness as the two sides sized each other up, neither trusting that the other had not done something unexpected. And then a shout and a crash. Everyone whirled round to see the Alchemist topple over backward, flailing at something none of them could see.

"Who's there?" he shouted, getting to his feet and smoothing his jacket down, enraged by being made fun of. Before he got any answers, Merlin stumbled as his staff was yanked from his hand, vanishing as it reached whatever had taken it.

"Show yourself, Anonymous Reader," Merlin said, his face white with anger.

"You ought to keep better track of your possessions." Milo's voice echoed from the other side of the courtyard as he reappeared with a pop, standing by the anvil, sliding a golden ring with a dark red stone from his finger.

"My ring," Merlin hissed. "You stole my ring."

"You never asked for it back," Milo said, "so I thought I'd keep hold of it for you, especially after we realized what it could do. You never know when invisibility might come in useful."

Milo was trying desperately to channel Tilly's bravery, Alessia's confidence, and Oskar's humor when he spoke to Merlin, even though his insides were roiling in panic. "And speaking of keeping track of your stuff," he said, "I would have thought these were being more carefully guarded." And, from behind his back, Milo pulled out *The Book of Books* and the Alchemist's book of fate. Merlin shot forward, but Milo steeled himself and yelled, "No!"

Merlin stopped, unsure for once.

"If you come any closer, I will imagine a fire more quickly than you could do anything, and both these books will be destroyed in moments. I'd be lying if I said that I knew what impact that would have, but I doubt it would be good, especially for you. So, Merlin, Mr. della Porta, would you please stay where you are, and if the rest of you could come over here? Quite quickly, please."

A small taste of fear sounded in Milo's last words, and Merlin and the Alchemist started forward, anger blazing in their eyes. Milo knew they would pounce at the first sign of weakness, and he was ready with a conjured flame that stopped both of them in their tracks.

"Very impressive," the Alchemist said. "You have clearly, once again, been underestimated, Mr. Bolt. I always knew you had great power. I am sure that we will be able to come to an excellent arrangement together."

"The time for deals is over," Milo said firmly as he passed the books to Tilly and Alessia. Tilly took the book the Fates had given her, and immediately imagined a flaming torch to keep Merlin and the Alchemist at bay. Alessia did the same.

"Well done, Tilly," her grandad whispered, putting a supportive hand on her shoulder. In the chaos, Merlin had clearly abandoned the spell that was stopping anyone from speaking.

"We can talk?" Horatio said. "Thank goodness for that. I have a lot to say, actually."

"Now isn't the time, Uncle," Milo said, and Horatio was stunned into silence.

"Lead on then, Milo," he said eventually. "I'm behind you."

"What exactly do you hope to achieve from this?" Merlin said. "This is a waste of my time. You have all shown you are not willing to actually harm us to achieve your ends."

"I'm not sure that's true," Horatio said. "Once I get the hang of this imagining business, I won't be as peaceable as these kids."

"Now, Horatio"—the Alchemist tried again with a placatory tone—"we've worked together for a very long time. I see no reason to be on opposite sides of this line."

"Because, at some point along the way, I got things very confused," Horatio said gruffly. "And I decided on some priorities that I realize now I got very out of order. I put the life of young Matilda here at risk, all to protect my train and my nephew, of course. Despite that, Matilda has shown herself to be willing to help me, which says it all."

He gave Tilly a nod, and she returned it solemnly. She knew that it was the closest she was ever going to get to an apology from Horatio, and she was more than happy to accept it. Sometimes people said sorry through what they did, not what they said.

"Oh, come now," said the Alchemist, laughing. "You'd do anything to protect the Quip and Milo. How about if we say that you two can return safely, and we'll leave you be, to smuggle your way around the world in peace?"

"Milo will not be permitted to leave," Merlin said.

"Very well," the Alchemist went on, looking distinctly irked. "Horatio, why don't you head off on your train? You've never cared that much for family, have you?"

"I don't think you're listening," Horatio said, his voice full of barely suppressed anger. "Don't you dare talk to me about my family after what you did to my mother."

"Ah, you heard, did you?" the Alchemist said. "Horatio, you know she would have betrayed you at the first whisper that she could have what she wanted. And, in fact, that's exactly what she did."

"That's beside the point," said Horatio.

"You have a funny understanding of family then," the Alchemist retorted.

"And you have a better one, do you?" Alessia spluttered, unable to contain herself anymore.

But the Alchemist just laughed. "I almost forgot you were here," he said.

Milo could see Alessia trying her best not to let his words

hurt her, even though he could see her lip wobble a little.

"I'm surprised you want to work together," Tilly said quietly, "when it comes down to it. Calliope told us everything—that you were the one, Merlin, who bound the magic of stories and imagination into the rules we all get tangled in. And, Mr. della Porta? All your work has been to rid yourself of the rules that he concocted and then made real. Without him, you would have had free rein over your own imagination anyway! *The Book of Books* won't help you. Have you even read it?"

"There has not been time yet," the Alchemist admitted. "We had to work out how to deal with all of you before I could sit and study it. But your words have no impact, Matilda. Yes, I want to free my own imagination, but you have not listened carefully to what I have been saying if you think I wish to extend that courtesy to everyone."

"This is no more than a rule book," Milo said, taking *The Book of Books* back from Alessia and opening it. "Just rules and lists and punishments and control. It has no true magic in it. The only power it has is what Merlin has given it, and the power it holds over him, sustaining him here."

As Milo turned the pages, taking in the ways that Merlin had limited imagination in order to hold sway over his legacy, he realized that the answer was actually very simple. First of all, he took Merlin's staff and cracked it over his knee. Merlin shuddered.

"That is no matter," he said. "It is but a way to channel my power. It is mainly for appearances."

But then Milo turned to the front of the book, hoping that everything he had learned about bookwandering and imagination from Tilly and Alessia and Oskar and his uncle and the Pages family would hold true. The first page read:

*Here are written the statutes of bookwandering, the laws created by Merlin the wizard, to contain the power of imagination for a greater purpose. The magic is bound to me, and to this Book.*

Milo took a deep breath and ripped the page from its binding, then held it up to the torch that Tilly was holding. Steeling himself one last time, he set it alight. It burned quickly, and Merlin shrieked in rage.

"You do not know what you are doing!" he yelled. "You do not know the power you are unleashing. You are destroying everything! Everything! Your legacy will be that you are the last bookwanderer!"

He strode forward, but as Milo ripped out the next few pages, the ones that stated that only a few readers would be able to access bookwandering magic to limit its power in the world, and set those on fire, Merlin stopped short, clutching at his chest in agony.

"You have limited bookwandering for too long!" Milo shouted. "Every reader should be able to travel within stories! I may be the last of your kind of bookwanderer, but I'm the first who will be truly free!"

He pulled out the next few pages, the ones that told bookwanderers to set up Underlibraries to bind Source Editions and control the flow of book magic, and held them to the flame. At this, Merlin stumbled to his knees.

"You cannot destroy me," he said. "I will last forever in the pages of the legends."

"And that is where you should always have stayed," Milo said. "You've taken more time than you were given to tell your story. You broke a circle to make an unceasing line, but I will tie its ends again."

"Geronimo, help me!" Merlin screeched, scratching at the stones in pain, trying to reach the Alchemist, who stepped away from him, looking repulsed at his desperation.

"I think that maybe it is time for you to go back to legend," he said with distaste. "And I will explore this brave new world where imagination is free for me to manipulate."

Tilly gave Milo a worried glance at that, but he was entirely focused on Merlin. As the last pages of *The Book of Books* were added to the heap of burning paper on the courtyard ground, Merlin accepted defeat. Kneeling on the ground, he looked up at Milo and nodded, closing his eyes.

"You have to admit," he said in a scratchy whisper, as the edges of him started to sparkle and glitter with book magic, "it was a very good tale."

And with that, he dissolved into iridescent dust on the air, returning to legend where he would endure but only as a circle of ink and paper and 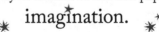 imagination.

## Meddling

"An excellent idea," the Alchemist said, kicking at the ash of *The Book of Books* with his fancy leather shoe. "He would have worked with no one, and you, Milo, have created a limitless playground. I am excited to see what world we will return to."

"It isn't one I think that you should go back to," Tilly said.

"Come now, there's no need to be uncivilized," the Alchemist said. "Look, I've spent several lifetimes trying to find *The Book of Books*, only to discover it contained very little of use and then have someone burn it in front of me, and I'm being very calm about it. Now, I wonder what will happen to this layer of Story that Merlin carved out now he's gone."

As if in answer, there was a rumbling underfoot.

"Aren't we in Arthurian legends?" Archie asked in concern.

"Not quite," Tilly replied. "We're in a version of them, but it's one Merlin made to hide in forever. We're not inside a book. I think this might be like when the Archive crumbled into nothingness."

"Right," Horatio said pragmatically. "We'd better get out then. Where's the Quip, Milo?"

"Uh, not here," Milo said awkwardly. "It's in Northumberland. Via Tintagel."

"So, how exactly do we get out?" Alessia asked. "Did we get rid of Merlin too soon?"

"Does the tree portal still work?" Oskar asked. "Is it still open without him, so we can get to Pages & Co.?"

"Let's hope so," Tilly said, and they ran from the shaking courtyard as the sky turned blood red.

"Where is this tree?" the Alchemist shouted. Tilly was ignoring the question of what to do with him for the moment, the rumbling ground taking up too much of her attention.

"I think it can be anywhere," Tilly said. "We just have to be able to summon it—and open it. Everyone hold on to each other and imagine Pages & Co." She grabbed her grandad with one hand and Oskar with the other, and thought desperately of being home. But there was a block, something that was working differently. She opened her eyes and realized the Alchemist was holding Alessia hard by the shoulder to stop them from leaving without him, but his power was interfering; his selfishness and the way he had tangled himself with imagination was blocking theirs.

"Let go!" Tilly yelled.

"And have you leave me here?" the Alchemist shouted back, over the ever louder rumblings and shakings. "Oh, I don't think so!"

"Can't you use your amazing powers to get us out somehow?" said Oskar. "What good is being attached to the world's imagination if you can't use it?"

"Everything is shifting because of your meddling," the Alchemist replied, letting his guard slip. "Your obsessions with freedom and choice have ruined everything. I will have to start all over again! But I will! Your imaginations will all be mine before long, I swear that to you. And, now I have a whole world full of bookwanderers to access, my power will be limitless before long, and you will all fuel it, whether you like it or not."

He yanked a petrified Alessia farther away from the rest of the group.

"You are not leaving without me," the Alchemist said. "Don't come any closer or you put Alessia in peril."

"She's your daughter," Archie said in disgust, and started toward the Alchemist, angrier than Tilly had ever seen him. "How dare you."

"Get out of my way, old man," the Alchemist said, and with a flash of venom in his eyes he sent a blast of light from his hand straight at Archie.

Everything seemed to go in slow motion as the light hit Archie directly in the center of his chest, and he toppled to one side.

# 37

N o!" cried Tilly as Grandad crashed to the ground in front of her.

The place on his jumper where the Alchemist's attack had hit him was blackened, and he was struggling to breathe.

# 38

Tilly took his head gently in her lap as his face turned pale. "Grandad, no, you can't leave me," she said. "I need you too much."

"Ah, Tilly," he said quietly. "It's okay. What a grand adventure I've had; not many people can say that. I'm so proud of you, my brave and curious and kind girl."

"Somebody do something!" Tilly shouted through her tears as the others knelt around him, but his pulse was fading, and his eyes were closing as the ground shook.

# 39

A feeling of utter despair overtook Tilly as she stared up at the Alchemist, who didn't look even slightly remorseful.

He shrugged. "I said that no one should come near me," he said icily. "I will be returning to Pages & Co. with you all, and I suggest you hurry up and work out how."

Tilly scrambled to her feet and went to run at him, but Oskar and Milo held her back.

"You can't," Milo said, tears also running down his cheeks. "We have to get home, and we can't risk Alessia's safety. Your family will help us work out what to do with him when we get back."

Tilly closed her eyes. Her mind was entirely full of deep, dark sadness—she felt as if she were drowning, like there was a great iron anchor holding her at the very bottom of the sea, where the water was inky and full of monsters.

# 4o

Oskar took Tilly's hand and she opened her eyes. "We need you to get us home," he said quietly. "I believe in you, Tilly Pages. And so did your grandad. Can you keep going? Just for a little bit longer?"

And then he gave her a huge hug, and Tilly felt the anchor pulled up toward the air, just a little. Just high enough that she could see the sky and start swimming upward herself. She wiped her eyes with her sleeve and breathed heavily. It was now or never, and the time for grief would come later. She stared steadily at the Alchemist, and the look on her face was enough to make him stumble backward. "I need Alessia," she said quietly and firmly.

"I said—" the Alchemist started, but then Alessia took matters into her own hands, kicking him in the shin at the same time as biting the hand holding her and squirming away.

"You little—" he hissed.

"I recommend that you keep quiet," Tilly said, "if you want to get home. Because you know as well as I do that we're the only way you leave here. Horatio—watch him."

Horatio didn't argue. He nodded and stood up, arms crossed, eyes fixed on the Alchemist.

# 41

Tilly gathered Oskar, Alessia, and Milo around her, forming a tight circle. They were all dirty and exhausted and tear-streaked.

"I know what we need to do," she said, putting down the Alchemist's heavy book of fate, bound in brass and iron. "I remembered the other similarity between the Archive and here. And that, in the end, Merlin and the Alchemist are not so different. Neither of them deserve a happy ending. Alessia, do you have the eitr?"

Alessia nodded, scrabbling in Rosa's backpack to find the vial. She gave it to Tilly and looked at her questioningly, but as she saw Tilly open the book of fate to the last page, a look of realization and determination came over her.

"Do you know what I'm going to do?" Tilly said.

"There or thereabouts," Alessia said. "Yes."

"Is that okay?" Tilly asked her. "He's your father. Even after everything, you get the final say."

Alessia took the tiny flowering wooden sword from her pocket and held it tight. She showed it to the others.

"I think my imagination gave me this to remind me of the treehouse, of Rosa, of everything she's taught me, and that, well, that I have a new family now," she said, a tear running down her cheek. "You must do what you must do. I'm ready."

# 42

Tilly gave Alessia's hand a squeeze, and the two girls knelt down next to each other.

"I wish I had a quill or a pen or something," Tilly said, before she and Alessia looked at each other and would have laughed if it weren't for the awfulness of the situation. She pulled the silver-tipped quill from her pocket, the one her imagination had given her.

"Looks like when we imagined what we needed, it wasn't swords in the end," Tilly said as Alessia carefully unscrewed the silver bottle of poison. "I got a quill, you got the reminder you needed, and Oskar, you got the hammer that helped free us."

"What about Milo?" Oskar asked.

"Oh, Milo has always had everything he needed," Alessia said simply, as though it were obvious. "I knew that the moment I met him." And she gave his hand a squeeze.

"Ready?" Tilly said, and the other three nodded. Tilly

dipped the quill in the poison, where it fizzed slightly but didn't dissolve, and she smoothed out the last page of the Alchemist's book of fate. They could hear him jostling and fussing and asking Horatio what the others were doing.

As Tilly started to write, she spoke. "This is the book of your fate," she began, and the others parted so the Alchemist could see her. "It was a gift to us because you have extended the thread of your life beyond what was set aside for you. You have used that life to steal power and control and make nothing good or kind for anyone but yourself. You would have enslaved the world's imagination for your own use. And so, Geronimo della Porta, your story is ending. This poison will make it so."

Tilly wrote the words as she spoke them, in eitr, on the pages of his fate.

# 43

As the Alchemist realized what Tilly was doing, he started pushing against Horatio to no avail. Tilly felt the shudders as he tried to use his imagination to intervene, but the other three were holding hands, imagining an impenetrable shimmering dome over her. And, very soon, the poison started to take effect, separating him from the influence he had stolen for too long.

"I bind your story so that no one will know or remember it," Tilly went on, shaking as she wrote, thinking of Calliope and trying to find the right words. She paused, for there was only one last thing to write.

"The End," Tilly scratched onto the rough paper, and the book **snapped shut** by itself and vanished.

# 44

The Alchemist stilled, staring at them in abject horror. He was clutching at himself in panic. Then, just as with Merlin, his edges started to blur and disappear. He aged as it happened, the years he had stolen being returned to him as the book magic he had hoarded left him. His fate was now sealed by the book, and his thread finally cut.

"You have stolen my life from me," he rasped.

"You stole that life," Oskar said.

"You stole our imaginations," Alessia said, tears tracking down the soot on her face.

"You were never good enough to be my daughter," he said as he faded.

"She's considerably too good to be your daughter," Horatio said.

"You are all . . . ridiculous," the Alchemist said. "You are too . . . too . . . good," he finished with a hiss of disgust. "And you . . ." He turned to Tilly, but speech left him, and he didn't get to deliver his last line.

Tilly would never know what he was trying to say, and she didn't care. His story had gone on long enough.

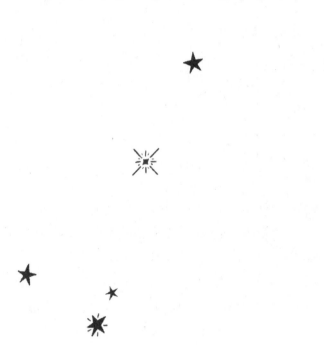

# 45

## A Twist of Fate

The five of them stood on the shaking ground.

Horatio bent down and tenderly picked up Archie's body.

"We need to get home," Oskar said gently, tears running down his own grimy cheeks. "I know this is awful, Tilly, but we have to go get that portal open."

Tilly tried to make her way through the horrified daze she was in, knowing Oskar was right. She stumbled forward, but couldn't focus her mind to start thinking about it.

Then Tilly felt Oskar take her hand, and Milo take the other. Alessia made them into a circle, a story of their own. In the center of the circle, a tiny shoot sprouted from the cracked and shaking ground, and as they watched, it grew and grew and grew, up toward the darkening sky. The four of them dropped their hands as the tree became too big to encircle, and then there was the outline of the door.

But before she could reach out and open the door in the tree, there was a pause in the tumult, and something bright caught Tilly's eye from above. She looked up, shielding her eyes, not able to work out what was coming toward her. It came gently, not like falling stones or branches, but floating like a feather or a . . . a page from a book.

It was a piece of parchment folded into four, and it was glowing ever so slightly. It landed on Archie's still body as he lay in Horatio's arms. Horatio put him gently down on the ground, head in his lap, as Tilly went to take the piece of paper. She unfolded it to see that it was being lit by a piece of shining gold thread inside. It floated from the folded paper and came to rest on Archie's chest. On the piece of paper, there were only two words and then three letters:

*A gift*, it read, and it was signed with the letters *G, L, & A.*

The thread hummed and glowed and vanished, seeming almost to melt into Archie, right where the blackened mark was. And then, with a cough and a frown, Archie Pages opened his eyes.

"A twist of fate," he said with a croak, reaching out for Tilly's hand. Tilly didn't even try to stop the tears of joy that were pouring down her cheeks now as she flung herself into his arms.

Horatio knelt beside them and put a gentle hand on Tilly's shoulder. She reluctantly let her grandad go, and Horatio helped Archie back up. The group approached the tree, and Tilly reached out and touched the handle carved into the wood. The door opened easily

and showed

them

the way

home.

# The Quip

Horatio Bolt sat in the engine room of the Sesquipedalian, keeping track of the levels of book magic. It was burning nicely, and so he sat back with his cup of coffee and his book. He'd been rereading *The Railway Children* for the first time since he was a child. For a long time, he'd thought he should put away such things, but these days he found great joy in reading books from all points of his life, reminding him of the person he had intended to become.

He was on his way back from a job tracking down a first edition of *Pride and Prejudice,* which was to be a wedding anniversary gift. He had discovered one abandoned in a box of books in the attic of an empty house, and he was going to restore it in the onboard bindery so that it could bring joy to a new reader's life.

He popped an extra orb of book magic into the engine, just in case, and leaned back happily. Just him and a book and the great expanse of imagination: most days it was all he wanted. And in an hour or so he'd reach his next destination, which was the only other thing he ever really needed.

# The Treehouse Library

"Are you ready for your uncle's visit?" Rosa asked Milo as he chopped up salad for dinner in the kitchen. A tiny flowering wooden sword was propped up behind the oven, still alive and growing months after it had first sprouted.

"I think so," Milo said. "I found a book I hope he'll like, if you don't mind me lending him something from the library?"

"Ah, your uncle has never been the most trustworthy library user," Rosa said with a smile. "But perhaps we can make an exception just this once. He only comes to visit every few months, so we've got to treat him. Let me go and check on how Alessia is doing up in the greenhouse. She's got some experiment on the go, and I've learned from past experience not to leave her for too long when she's got a theory to prove, if the three of us want a treehouse to live in for much longer."

She headed up the stairs, leaving Milo to his own thoughts, which these days were more content than he'd ever imagined possible. In the end, it had been the simplest arrangement in the world; he had no desire to be on the move all the time on the Quip, and Horatio had made it quite clear that he was more than content to be left to his own devices—most of the time.

Rosa had said that she'd be very keen for more company, and that they could call themselves apprentices, or family, as they fancied. Given what Rosa had had to come to terms with about the truth of *The Book of Books*, she had a lot of new research to do into imagination, which Alessia was eagerly helping her with.

Occasionally Milo and his uncle went for a drive on the Sesquipedalian, just the two of them, where they drank strong tea with roughly made sandwiches, and Horatio told him stories of their family.

Milo went to check how the roasted butternut squash was coming on as he heard the whistle of the Quip arriving by the lake.

"He's here!" he called up to Alessia and Rosa, who made their way down to the kitchen, ready for dinner.

# Pages & Co.

"Are we all done with dinner?" Grandma said, and Tilly, her grandad, and Bea all nodded. Bea started to clear the plates as Grandma put the remains of the chocolate roulade in the fridge, the evening light catching the Tintagel Castle fridge magnet.

It had been nine months since they'd defeated Merlin and the Alchemist, and destroyed *The Book of Books*. Things had changed a lot, and the Underlibraries were all having to work out their purpose now that the magic of bookwandering was not controlled by rules and limits. Amelia Whisper had stayed on as Head Librarian and spent a fair amount of time doing her own research into imagination, but the British Underlibrary was also talking about whether there was a way to open their doors to more readers now that anyone could bookwander. Oskar had been helping Amelia work out some ideas, as well as helping to build the Underlibrary's graphic-novel collection. It did mean that Tilly's bookwandering was not so different from anyone else's, now that no one had to worry about getting lost in the

Endpapers, and she found that she was quite content about that.

"Bea, I'd love to chat to you about the summer party," Grandma said. "So, Archie, why don't you and Tilly make some hot chocolates and drink them in front of the fire?"

"An excellent plan," Archie said, and he and Tilly made their perfect hot chocolate, with just the right number of marshmallows, and carried them through to the sofa by the fire. Pages & Co. was closed for the evening, with just a lamp for reading glowing by the sofa and the flickering light of the fire burning in the chimney. The portal to Merlin's hideaway had been closed off, just to be on the safe side.

"What shall we read tonight?" Archie said as Tilly snuggled into his side. "*Anne of Green Gables* perhaps? Or something new?"

"No, I'm in the mood for an old favorite," Tilly said, reaching for the book on the table and giving it to her grandad.

"A very good choice," he said as he opened the cover and started to read.

But we will leave them to their book now. Let us head to the door, where the "Closed" sign swings, and open and shut it ever so quietly so we do not disturb them. You can still see them through the window, Tilly and her grandad, lit by the light of the fire, a story unfolding in front of them.

## Epilogue
## After the End

**A**nd that is where we leave Pages & Co., reader.

But what's that? Do you feel something strange in the pit of your stomach, like the feeling when you go over the top of a roller coaster? Do you hear the click-clack of a world building itself around you? Can you smell something on the air? Something smoky and sweet, almost like marshmallows toasting on a bonfire? Hold on tight, bookwanderer. For when you are a reader, there is always a new adventure about to start.

## ~~THE END~~

*The Beginning*

# Book Magic

In the first Pages & Co. book, Grandad tells Tilly that bookshops are like a map of the world, and this applies to libraries too. My books are a celebration of the particular magic of bookshops and libraries, and I've been lucky to have a reading life shaped by them.

My earliest library memory is when I was six and I finished the school reading scheme. This meant I was allowed to go and choose my own reading book from the library. Even though it was really just a cupboard full of books, in my memory the shelves stretched up into the sky, and it felt like the world had been opened up to me. I was fortunate to have proper libraries in all my schools—something that is absolutely vital to fight for.

Sadly I didn't grow up in a bookshop, but my grandma and grandad were a huge part of my relationship with books, just like for Tilly. Whenever my little sister and I visited them in the Scottish Borders, there would always be a book on our pillows chosen from their local bookshop. And our local book-shop at home was the beautiful Waterstones Newcastle (the big staircase up the center of Pages & Co. is inspired by it!).

When I was older, I spent hours in the beautiful old library at the University of Birmingham, which is where I decided to become a librarian myself. I ended up working as a school librarian for nearly five years and saw first-hand the incredible impact that libraries and books can have on young people.

And now, Pages & Co. has found readers across the world because of the incredible booksellers and librarians who have championed it. There's not enough pages to list them all, but they are all fueled by book magic and make that map of readers stronger and richer every day. After all, to read is to wander, and bookshops and libraries are the places to set our compasses.

# Acknowledgments

H ere we are at the end of Pages & Co., and there are so many people who have helped me get to this point.

Thank you to my agent, Claire Wilson, a constant source of wisdom, kindness, and joy—thank you for seeing the very first spark of bookwandering magic and believing in it. Thank you to everyone at RCW, in particular Safae El-Ouahabi and David Dunn.

Thank you to my editor, Nick Lake, who inherited the series partway through but has always understood what book-wandering is all about, and has helped me guide it to the ending I always wanted. I truly love working together, thank you. And thank you to my previous editors, who all helped make Pages & Co. what it has become—thank you, Lizzie Clifford, Sarah Hughes, and Rachel Denwood.

Thank you to everyone at my publisher, HarperCollins Children's Books, for your care and talent. Thank you, Cally Poplak, Megan Reid, Jess Dean, Ellie Curtis, Isabel Coonjah, Elisa Offord, Alex Cowan, Laura Hutchison, Elorine Grant,

Carla Alonzi, Hannah Marshall, Jane Baldock, Deborah
Wilton, Nicole Linhardt-Rich, Jane Tait, Samantha Lacey, and
everyone at HCCB. Thank you also to HCCBers past—Louisa
Sheridan, Julia Sanderson, Samantha Stewart, Tina Mories,
and Jo-Anna Parkinson.

Thank you to my foreign publishers, in particular to
Cheryl Eissing and Tessa Mesicheid and the team at Philomel
in the US.

Thank you to Marco Guadalupi for your beautiful illustrations and the care you take in bringing the world of Pages &
Co. to life—I'm so grateful. And thank you to Paola Escobar for
your wonderful work on the first three books.

Thank you to every teacher, bookseller, librarian, and
blogger who has read, recommended, or championed the
series—it would not have found its readers without you, and
I am endlessly appreciative of everything you do to get books
into the hands and hearts of young readers. Thank you to Mr.
Weir, my A-level English teacher, who put so many books in
my hands and heart.

Thank you to my friends for your support/patience/love/
joy. Special thanks to my author friends, and in particular Katie
Webber and our never-ending conversation.

Thank you to my family—my mum and dad and my
sister, Hester. I love you so much. This book is dedicated to
my grandad, who is the inspiration for Tilly's grandad, but
I was lucky to have been loved by four amazing grandparents

who I miss very much. Thank you also to the Cottons/Colliers/Bishops/Rices—I am so lucky to be part of your family.

Thank you always to Adam, my best reader and my best person. I love you, okay!

And finally, thank you to every bookwanderer, young and old, who knows that imagination is real and powerful magic.